Book 3
Chronicles of the Martlet

I0571189

The Assassin's Twisted Path

Written by
Elizabeth Guizzetti

Edited by Joe Dacy
Cover and Interior Illustrations by Elizabeth Guizzetti

This is a work of fiction. Names, characters, businesses, places, events and incidents are products of the author's imagination or used in a fictitious manner. Any resemblance to actual persons, living or dead, or actual events is purely coincidental. (Also weird. I mean really this book is about a group of elves.)

Printed in the United States of America

Paperback ISBN-13: 978-0999559840
EBook ISBN-13: 978-0-9995598-5-7

This book is for all the folks who read this book...

Seven Populated Realms protected by the Guild

Cannik (Can nik)
Watery Realm of the vodnik

Daouail (Da o wail)
Realm of the Daosith

Dynion (Di nee on)
Realm of the humans

Fatidel (Fat i del)
Realm of the Fates

Fairhdel (Fair del)
Realm of the Fairsinge

Larcia (Lar see a)
Realm of the dwarves

Si Na (See Na)
Realm of the telchine
*Uttalassus (Ut ta lass us)
Technically within the Realm of Si Na.
Land of the gnomes

Realms not within the Guild

Risford (Rise Ford)
Realm of the Giants

Widae (Wed ae)
Realm of Dragons

Uncharted Realms

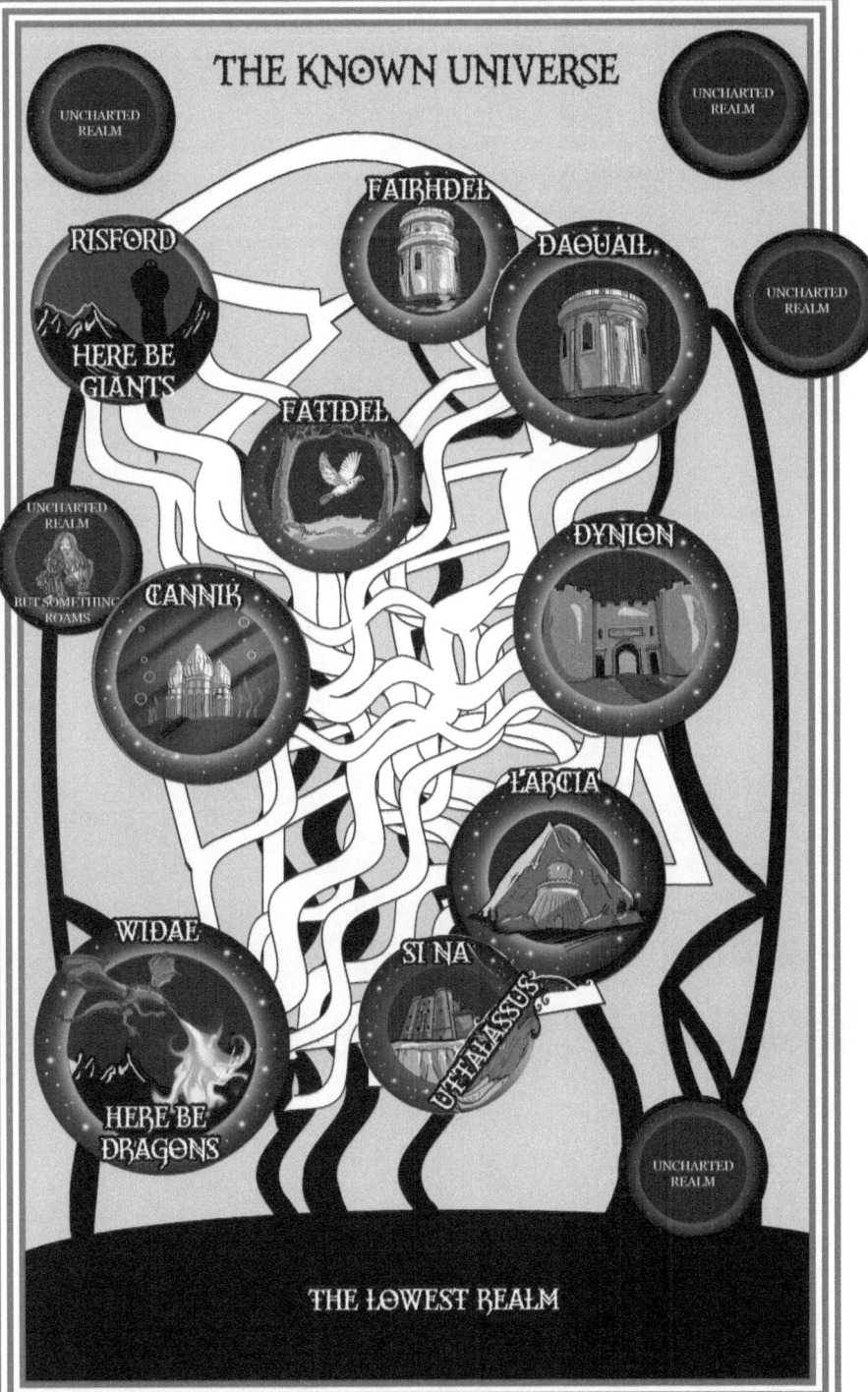

The Assassin's Twisted Path

Chapter 1
Upon the Expanse

THE ECHOING CALL OF THE CAPTAIN'S orders and stomping feet resounded over the newly-recognized Lord Roark, the Martlet of House Eyreid. He glanced out the InterRealm ship's porthole. The crescent-shaped edge of Dynion loomed among the mists of the Expanse.

Beside him, Lady Byronia, the Martlet of House Silba, sighed deeply, the pinch on her ivory brow proclaimed her sorrow as she stroked her tri-pointed ear —a terrible habit from childhood. She never spoke of her errands, but Roark could see they rested heavily upon her shoulders. Even with her grim manner, she had been an agreeable traveling companion; she had listened to stories and played hafal long in the night. A dear friend of his sister's, she had done nothing to arouse suspicion, but he didn't know if he could trust her. However, Roark was confident he could best her in sword-to-sword combat if necessary.

Searching for words of comfort, he clasped his hand to her wrist and met her sapphire eyes; not even the Expanse could match their depths. She had peerless gifts in diplomacy, but by her darkening attitude, Roark was reasonably sure she had been sent to Dynion on an assassination mission.

"Byrony," he said, using her childhood name in their mother tongue. "We do what we do for peace."

"Gods, you're young."

Byronia was only twenty-three summers to his eighteen, so he replied, "So are you."

"I'll be in the vicinity of Denwort for a few days, perhaps longer. Do you think Mister Candlewick would allow me to visit? I wish to remain friends. So many will be lost," she said.

Will be lost? Under Roark's tunic, the ruby-colored quartz pendant of wisdom shivered. "Why do you speak thus?"

"I've foreseen the possibilities many times. The future overwhelms my courage. Uncle Corwin bade me open my mind; I wish I hadn't taken that advice."

Roark pulled her from the porthole to the built-in table where the steward had set grapes, cheese, and olives. She allowed herself to be led and sat on the upholstered bench.

Roark took care not to raise his voice. "Enough riddles. Will you kill me for practicing the forbidden arts?"

Byronia's eyes opened wider, but her voice was without emotion. "If I had your contract, I would've just killed you here and asked the sailors to toss your body into the Expanse." She pressed her index finger into his brow. "Uncle told me your mind is open too; haven't you looked to the future?"

Roark didn't want to remember the future he had seen. "Somewhat."

"I had hoped ... you had seen too." She fiddled with a loose grape, rolling it against the platter. "Not even Corwin has seen what I have. Alana only glimpsed the smallest truth of it." Her eyes grew wild as they looked through him and into a destiny he couldn't see. She lowered her voice. "Be careful whom you trust."

The InterRealm ship jostled as it landed onto Dynion's northern sea. She met his eyes again. Her lips trembled. "When I move beyond the Seven Realms, you must keep the future."

"What are you talking about?"

Byronia spoke fast as if her spiraling words raced against the sailors as they docked in Port Denwort's deep harbor. "The pre-Schism had no autonomy. Technology made decisions for you in the name of efficiency and comfort, while making you believe you had control. It was a false paradise. The Guild keeps us free, but this is no paradise either. So many suffer because we're falling into entropy. This entropy precipitated famine, and the famine created the resurgence of slavery. Some of the old ways should not have re-risen. Why did we not learn from the Schism?

"Worse, entropic species are weak and ripe for conquering. I'll hold them back, but you must see to the future."

"You're talking in circles."

"Please, there's not much time."

He struggled to find a comforting response, yet not bind himself. "I'll do what I can."

Byronia flinched. His attempt had failed. She was too gifted in diplomacy to be fooled by any non-answer.

The steward called.

Byronia pumped his hand up and down in farewell. "I hope that in time, you will be more of a Martlet than you are now."

He wanted to point out all the times she had been less of a Martlet, but before a single word escaped his lips, she exited the cabin. Her blonde braid sparkled in the sun before she went below to the stable deck.

He waited until he was sure she was gone before he finished dressing, gathered his own gear and went below to the stable deck to collect Jaci.

※

3

Port Denwort
in the Realm of Dynion

SEPARATED FROM HIS DOUR AND APPARENTLY half-mad companion, Roark found a ride through the bustling, shop-lined streets of Port Denwort—a good enough reason to wear his fine clothes and house colors instead of drab traveling woolens. He relished watching humans of common blood incline their heads as he rode past on his majestic black mare. Though he did not prefer women, he adored the attention of two silk-clad human maidens of the merchant class who batted their eyes at his Fairsinge beauty. The girls seemed fragile things under their youthful, powdered, alabaster cheeks. Soon they would lose their loveliness. They would either die old or die young.

As would he. How many years would it be until all that was left of Lord Roark, the 38th Martlet of House Eyreid, was the portrait on his House's wall which would fade until some great-great nieces or nephews would hire a new artist to restore it? Perhaps that was what Byronia was rambling about. He shuddered; thinking of his own nightmares.

His majestic Jaci would die before him. His beloved aunt Alana, his parents, sister, brothers, and all his friends—Eohan, Kian, Seweryn, Kajsa, Doriel, and even the sanity-challenged Byronia—would all die. Their souls would disappear from the Seven Realms, walk the Long Road to the Lowest Realm while their bodies putrefied. Roark had seen many dead. All of them had been just dead, except one.

He had not forgotten the maze of stone houses and neat hedgerows to the small cottage on the hill. Chamomile buds trembled in the windowboxes

4

concealing what lay inside the curtains. He dismounted and knocked on the heavy red door where the only dead who walked lived.

The lich peeked out of the small window. His charcoal-lined obsidian eyes opened wide, and a gruesome smile exposed his yellowed teeth and blackened gums as he exclaimed, "Roark, my lad, it's good to see you."

"Hello, Mister Candlewick. I wasn't sure you'd remember me," Roark said.

"I could never forget the taste of your blood. How is your aunt? Still chasing after worthless slaves?" Edar opened his door and motioned for him to enter.

Roark noted the new blue silken robes that hung on the lich's withered frame and wondered what Edar traded for it: a potion, a secret, another slave bled of health? Inside, the reception room was clean, but Roark felt the oppressive darkness at the edges of the room. He forced a smile to his face. "Yes."

"Your aunt wastes her life on the unworthy. Please sit, my lad."

"I am Lord Roark now," Roark said and sat upon the chair which Edar offered.

"How nice for you," Edar said.

Roark declined to answer the lich's needling, especially since the undead human still followed human niceties of the northern providence. The lich set bread studded with currants on the table and put on a pot over the stove for herbal tea—chamomile and lavender by its smell.

"You look well," Edar said. "And in the spring of youth. Are you injured?"

"No." Roark took a sip of tea, confident Edar wouldn't poison him since he cared so deeply for the bodily fluids of his person.

Edar's face took on a look of concern. "Is Lady Alana injured?"

"Not that I know."

"She foolishly refused the last potion I offered. A bit of blood from her pretty friend and we both might have been young for weeks!"

Byronia's frightened expression rose in his mind; he pushed it down. "As my aunt informed me, but I gave my blood willingly; Byronia did not."

"You're taken with her?"

"The lady is an inseparable friend to my sister and was to my late cousin and often kind to me; I'm glad to call her my friend."

"Friendship might become more."

"I enjoy the company of men, and as I am thirdborn, it hardly matters for the bloodline." Roark returned to the true subject. "Your potion worked marvelously for healing and strength. Wounds closed quickly, but the visual side-effects did not last."

"Yes, and it depends upon the donor and the amount ingested. You were a fine donor. My potion made me appear alive for a hundred days. I even left the house several times."

"Alana sipped hers as needed. Her sword arm grew strong and reflexes quick. It was amazing." Roark chose his next words carefully. "When we found Kian, he was quite ill. Alana gave him the rest of her potion."

"Wasted the potion, you mean."

"Alana didn't consider it wasteful. Kian completely recovered. That is why, Mister Candlewick, I want you to teach me. Necromancy is an exhilarating science."

"Not one condoned by the Guild, Lordling."

There it was. He might have told Edar that House Master Corwin had secretly condoned his research, but the quartz shocked him with an uncomfortable energy as it warned of the danger. *Don't give Edar any ideas about Corwin or me. Corwin would see him dead.*

Edar is dead, Roark thought back.

6

The quartz zapped him. *I might be considered proof of betrayal since you liberated me from another necromancer.*

Roark spoke a deeper truth. "I don't care about the Guild. It pays well, but the hypocrisies are many. If I were from a wealthier House, I wouldn't soil my hands with them."

Edar pointed at the wooden broach of an eagle holding a smaller golden swift which fastened Roark's cloak. "And that?"

"My mother still rules; my aunt still wanders. It will be many years until much is expected of me."

"Odd for a young man to care about necromancy. You're what? Seventeen?"

"Eighteen summers," Roark said.

"Still so very young. Does Lady Alana know you are here?"

Humans completed their apprenticeships in their early twenties, so he took care to mention it. "Alana released me from my apprenticeship, but yes, she does. I've seen death. I'll be killing another in three weeks. I've a recurring vision of the Long Road where all the dead walk. Nightmares and idle thoughts haunt me."

"Why is that?" Edar asked.

"I found happiness in Eohan and Kian's companionship, but see the deceit in common elfkin beliefs."

"Such as?"

"The priests say if I live by valor and goodness, I'll be resurrected as a Noblewoman's son, however, if two people as good-hearted as my friends might be born commoners and made slaves through no fault of their own, how can I believe what the priests say? How do I know what I'll become if I step into the Waters of Resurrection? The mists of the Expanse are chaotic."

A shadow of wretchedness drifted onto Edar's

face. "You obviously expect to come and go at your convenience?"

"The Guild's convenience, but yes."

"What do I get from this arrangement?"

"I expected you shall want some of my blood," Roark said.

Edar smiled. "For regular donations, I will teach you everything I know. Now don't worry, I won't bleed you too quickly. I've learned patience in my death."

"Good. I'll need to water my horse and find her housing. Is there a nearer stable than the market square?"

"Mayor Kleidmacher would be honored to stable a lordling's horse, but he'll ask your aunt for a favor sometime." Edar gesture over his shoulder. "I keep a bed in my mother's old room. It's clean ... and yes, Lordling, there's a lock on the door."

Roark wasn't sure how Alana might feel about that, but she'd traded her blood for a safehouse with Edar. His mother and father needn't know or understand the risk. "I'll return within the hour then. Need anything from the shops?"

"The dairywife comes 'round in the morning, but if it isn't too much trouble ... " Edar scribbled a few items on a spare piece of parchment, the back of which held a list of herbs, and handed Roark a few coins. "Buy some sausages or chops if any are fresh. It's been so long since I broke bread with another."

After a quick turn around the market and a flirtatious exchange with a human rentboy, Roark rode to the mayor's stately stone house flanked by two stone towers, only three houses away from Edar's little cottage. The grandfatherly Mayor Kleidmacher of Port Denwort, who was also the chief spokesman of the Silk Merchants Guild, greeted him warmly, was glad to see Roark in good health, and inquired about Alana.

It was hard to meet the old man's eyes when the

oversized tapestry called to him. Brown paths of thread led to a central design of intertwined swirls of rich blue surrounding two black seraphim centered within an orb within an orb within an orb. Below the circle patterns, sparkling white and blue waterfall hid figures of every species within in the waves. The Lowest Realm.

As Edar said he'd be, the mayor was thrilled to house a "newly promoted Elf Lord's horse" and offered to house Roark who declined. After securing Jaci, Roark returned to Edar's cottage. He set the fruit on the table and meat in the cold box on the north wall.

"I'm here, Lord Roark," the lich called.

Roark followed the voice to the rear of the house where Edar arranged lavender and wolfsbane upon the mattress which lay on a welcoming, primitively carved oak bed. The room was dressed simply, but well for a family of the merchant's class. Besides the oak bed, an oak chest lay on the east wall. A washing pot lay on a small table, and a chamber pot was in the corner and had a folding door to the outside for emptying. Edar placed a crisp linen sheet with a slight brown smudge over the herbs and mattress. "I hope you'll be comfortable."

Roark touched the smudge. "Headwound?"

"Fear not. It wasn't Lady Alana's blood. Just a bit left on her scalp from misadventure."

"Auntie's entire life is a misadventure," Roark muttered.

Edar chuckled as he smoothed the sheets. "A maid comes in every second day to keep the place neat. She will also draw baths but is not to be touched. She's a good servant."

Roark wasn't sure if Edar meant she wasn't to be harvested for blood or molested, but the vows of his station and moral code prohibited him from doing either. He said, "I understand."

Edar opened the window and smiled sadly. "My

mother had a nice prospect of the garden. Like you, the aging of a beloved mentor spiked my interest in necromancy."

When Edar spoke of his mother, Roark could almost see the human he once was.

"Do you need rest? I've much to show you," Edar said.

Roark set his saddlebags on the oak chest. "I can start immediately, if it pleases you, Mister Candlewick."

"It does, Lord Roark," Edar replied with true eagerness in his voice and step. "But please call me Edar. Death has claimed many of my friends."

"Please call me Roark as my aunt does."

"Then change from those fine clothes, Roark, and let's begin."

✻

Chapter 2
Port Denwort
in the Realm of Dynion

ROARK FOLLOWED THE LICH DOWN THE stone cellar stairs to his laboratory which smelled of rot, vinegar, and lemons. A damp breeze brushed his cheeks, and a repetitive clicking resounded in the darkness, but he couldn't see from where it originated until Edar lit candle lamps to illuminate the dead human in the middle of the room. On a large metal table, gray bloating skin drained of life into a bucket below. A three-bladed fan connected to a set of bellows spanned most of the south wall. To the north, wooden cupboards filled with ceramic jars of organs and eyeballs lined the wall. Empty beakers, scales, and ceramics of all shapes and sizes lined the east wall. On the west was another workbench with thick dusty tomes, writing utensils, parchment, and strange contraptions.

"You aren't squeamish?" Edar asked.

"No. My aunt bade me dissect Fairsinge and Vodnik corpses so I'd know where the organs are."

"Really? I've never seen the inside of a Fairsinge or a Vodnik! Is that standard Guild training?"

"Standard Alana training. Are all your specimens human?"

"Yes. This one was a thief, hung not two days prior. The mayor's man cut him down for the ... " he gestured below his waist. "Male enhancements I make."

"The mayor needs such things?"

"An old man hanging onto the breath of life needs many remedies. And so many remedies and poisons come from the pickled organs of an evil man. Come, I've so much to show you." Edar sliced a piece of hairy flesh off the corpse and brought it to his stacked lenses on the workbench. "Look, look at this."

Roark peeked through the stacked lenses. It took a moment to clear his eyes, but he couldn't believe what he observed. Millions of tiny cells intertwined. "The skin doesn't look whole ... "

"None of us are whole. I have seen my skin and Kian's. Yours is the same, but I rarely have an elfkin to experiment on. Kian was the last."

"I've a scar on my chest. I'll reopen it for you. Perhaps, I could bring you some specimens from my Guild work. I can't tell you where I'm bound, but if we study the differences between intelligent species, we might find the answers we seek."

Edar's eyes sparkled. "Yes, yes."

The lich walked to his cupboard and removed a jar of some unspeakable component. "Roark will like this," he muttered to himself. "And this one." He returned, cranked the lenses higher in their base, set the first jar inside, and lifted the lid. "See this? It's a human liver."

A foul, acrid smell filled Roark's nostrils, but in the mass of decomposing flesh, he witnessed a world of heavy striations, circles and parabolas, and tiny dark specks that he could not see with his bare eyes. "Amazing. It's its own tiny Realm."

"My thoughts exactly. Would you like to see the human heart next?" Edar asked. "I can't wait to show you." He removed the liver jar and replaced it with another.

"Without the lenses, a human heart looks much like a Fairsinge or Daosith heart, but we have four ventricles, not the two."

"How wonderful!" Edar clapped his hands together and went to the cabinet for another few jars, muttering about what Roark might like to see next as if Roark could not hear him.

He would have never guessed a lich might be lonely. That would be something he must plan for if he wished to live forever.

※

EDAR RETIRED TO HIS BED, BUT ROARK WAS unable to stay still. He had learned so much already, but nothing to send to Corwin. It bothered Roark he didn't disclose that a Guild House Master had shown interest in necromancy. Now it was too late to speak of it. The lich would believe Roark had deceived him.

Roark had never experienced such conflict when working with Alana. Her noble name was bound by noble deeds, but even she lived by telling people only what they needed to know.

He quietly slipped into the back garden, but his brain—or perhaps the blood red quartz hidden under his undertunic—called him to wander. He was a man now, but he was also Edar's apprentice and needed to remain in the man's good graces.

He reclined across the garden bench, slipped his finger around the gold chain and exposed the pendant. He pierced his finger with a blade and dripped blood onto the stone. It drank hungrily.

You have the curse. Use it, the quartz whispered.

"It always comes to the curse, doesn't it?"

The curse is why I am happy you liberated me. I was separated from my family and hung about a stupid neck.

He carefully slipped the pendant back under his

shirt and shifted his weight for comfort. He released his spirit from his physical form.

Port Denwort was a human city, but in such a large port with ships coming and going, peoples of all species moved about the pubs. The market was closed, but wagons circled the square. The merchants tucked soundly into their carts. In pairs, guards strolled along the main streets. Stopping into a pub or two, they received a pint on the house.

The ship which he and Byronia had arrived in, rocked upon the sea, tied to the docks. As soon as his mind imagined her name, his spirit transported to a sprawling plantation where a dark Byronia-shaped silhouette hid among fruit-laden brambles. Beyond the orchard stood a great brick house, several tatty wooden structures, and another brick building where seven men, armed with knives and thick ropes, played cards with no understanding how close they were to danger.

Roark briefly wondered why she was there. Perhaps she was still rescuing slaves. But then why was she wearing the Weave? The black Guild fabric was created for ease of movement and silence once it hugged the skin. It was made for assassinations.

Byronia's errand isn't my business. Learning how to defeat death was his business. He returned to his body.

Nausea swept over him. He missed how, when he was a boy, his aunt would place a cool cloth on his brow.

His lips flaked. Light punctured his retinas. The songs of crickets filled his ears, followed by a howling scream. Roark took a step on a long desert and broke through the thin crust spread across thick goopy muck. The heat of an unseen sun beat upon him and the evaporated liquid formed a mist. Every step, he stumbled through the crust. Salt flew in the air.

Stone columns rose from the plain. On top of the

pillars lay an orange, leafless tree covered in large hairy pods with white birds, bats, and small rodents asleep in the branches. Another scream and growling echoed from behind him.

Millions of insects, several rodents and other small animals, a few vodnik, humans, and elfkin—all rotting flesh—lurched and swayed towards the Lowest Realm. Telchine shed particles of clay and the dwarves lost pebbles of stone with each step.

Roark's only comfort was that this time his cousin, Saray, was nowhere in sight. She must have passed from the Long Way to the Lowest Realm. Roark wanted to say a prayer for her, but he didn't believe it would help. Instead, he chanted his living friends' names as a mantra: *Alana, Eohan, Kian, Byrony, Kajsa, Doriel, Seweryn ...* he added *Edar* to the list. He thought of their faces with the hope they would not leave him in this terrible place. His research would ensure that they never came along this Way either.

※

Chapter 3
On the outskirts of Port Denwort
in the Realm of Dynion

CLOTHED IN THE WEAVE, BYRONIA SAT hidden amongst the brambles of the berry plantation and waited for the correct moment. On Corwin's command, she must collect illegal technology before the humans shattered the centuries-long relative peace shared between dwarves, elfkin, gnomes, humans, telchine, and vodnik. Humans were an inquisitive species. They did not know this technology brought the falling of the Veil.

Each step brought her future closer, but she categorized all her option—including suicide and self-mutilation. It didn't matter. How naive she had been to think the curse could change her path for the better. Foresight allowed her to squash fear of battles, disgust of assassinations, and the darkness which blighted the Seven Realms because she knew that she would live beyond that night. In eight years, her path would open. She would stand witness to wonders and terrors. The other option was to take her consort and run to the furthest reaches of Fairdhel. She might live a commoner's life until Corwin's assassin found her.

She observed the seven human overseers to ascertain their schedule, habits, and favorite haunts. She even learned some gossip from the slave quarters about how the elfkin slaves had gained their freedom via two angels from the lowest Realms. She wished she could free all those who lived in bondage without fault of their own. She understood the need for criminals to lose their freedom, but the average poor citizen who was sold or stolen? She silently let these thoughts consume her until the last light was extinguished in the slave corridor and the overseer's barracks went dark.

Byronia waited until the moon dropped one finger-width in the sky before sprinting down the row of harvested berry bushes to the back of an old barn. She slunk around to the front, careful not to step in the moonlight and cast a shadow. A single guard sat on a stool in front of the barn door, his back leaning against the wooden slats.

She tossed a rock over his head. It landed with a small clack. He faced the sound. She sprinted towards him with her dagger outstretched and sliced open his throat. He gurgled out his last breath. She dumped him onto the ground, picked the lock and dragged him inside the barn.

In the darkness, seven mechanical bulls stood unmoving. Beside them was a work table covered in tools. She stuffed them into her bag. Then found a box of gears and washers and took them as well.

She ran her hands over the first bull's enormous muscular body. At the base of its neck, she found a lever she'd observed earlier. She pressed it towards the head. The motor ticked and reverberated, and the bull slowly grumbled to life. She turned on each one and yoked them together. She secured the body of the guard onto the back of one of the bulls before she herded them south.

As if they were living beasts, they snorted and swayed their heavy metal horns as they moved. Every heavy footfall clanked and clopped on the stone ground. She hoped they didn't wake anyone. She didn't kill lightly. She drove them to her cache where her saddled mare, Joy, grazed among the long grasses.

The mechanical bulls kept pace with her horse's trot as they moved further south, deeper into the forest. Every few hundred feet, Byronia would dismount and sweep their hoofprints away until they came to a stone hillside. She led her horse, who in turn led the bulls up the embankment until they came to a tall cliff face where a small occupied Guild safehouse stood. She knocked on the door.

An old human woman answered, "I'm coming; I broke a hip last winter, not that you'd care."

Byronia cupped her hand slightly in front of her chest and made a sweeping gesture. "Of course, I'd care."

The woman responded in kind and glanced over Byronia's shoulder. "You claim to be House Master's Corwin's daughter?"

"I claim to be his niece. His daughter fell in a great battle."

"Ah. My condolences. It's hard to remember all the elfkin relations," she said. "Time for tea, my lady? I've a nice citrus blend from Si Na."

"Perhaps, on my way back? I believe the House Masters are waiting."

"Shouldn't keep them waiting then, but I look forward to your return, my lady."

"As do I."

The old woman opened a closet door and threw some cloaks to the floor which covered a crank. She turned the crank, and a passage opened a wall.

Within the passage, a vortex of blinding light spun. Byronia led the bulls to the vortex one by one, their heavy horns flashing with the light before disappearing into the Guild House. After each one was through the gate, Byronia ushered Joy through. Unlike the mechanical bulls, Joy danced with fear before she allowed herself to be escorted through the vortex.

✳

Guild House of Norcrest in the Realm of Dynion

THE NIGHT BREEZE CHILLED HER WET BODY as Byronia stepped out of the crystal lake and onto the meadow. Beside her, Joy shook the water from her mane, soaking her all the more. Several human and elfkin guards and two dwarf mechanics welcomed her. Byronia made the common sweeping Guild greeting. They did the same. The mechanics gathered each bull and herded them west to the vault. A Daosith asked Byronia a few questions about Joy's care before leading her to the stables.

A hooded human approached, saluted in kind, and accompanied her into the Guild House. Thick grasses pulled at her tired legs, but the immense stone house soaring up the hillside offered shelter from the night breeze. A young Fairsinge apprentice, her brown braids flying, hurried over with fresh clothing. "I'll have your weave dried for you, milady. I'm here to care for House Master Corwin's needs; he bids me to care for you."

Byronia didn't recognize her from a noblehouse, she might not be an apprentice, but the daughter of one of the Guild Trades. If so, Corwin probably barked at the girl, so Byronia ensured she thanked her. She peeled the wet weave from her body and accepted the fresh robe.

Her footfalls silent against the stone floor, she followed the girl down a long, blue corridor with black numbered doors and a stained-glass skylight, which would have created dancing colors in the day, but with the night sky behind it was dim. The girl pointed at a door and then disappeared.

Byronia knocked. A human woman with the dark coloring typical to the Dynion's equatorial region opened the door to a sprawling windowless cell. Her gray curls created a halo around her withered face, but her wrinkles cast her expression in a perpetual mischievous grin. "Welcome, Journeywoman Byronia," Jaren said. "We've a nice new brew, can I offer you a pint?"

As with every time she met Jaren Oweleye, she thought how nice the human House Master seemed compared to her uncle, but one didn't become a House Master on kindness.

"Please," she said.

As with all Guild strategy rooms, the exact measurements were as elusive as the walls withdrew into dim gloom. As she stepped toward the center, the murkiness parted enough to see the outline of a massive oaken table and seven guild master's thrones where two were occupied with aged representatives of their respective species.

Her uncle, Corwin, the House Master of the Olentir Guild House, rose from his chair while Gabena Longroot, the Larcian Dwarfkin of the Malraindom Guild House, remained seated and poured Byronia a cup.

Corwin's habitual white linen robes moved as if he was surrounded by ether. His pale, deep wrinkles and piercing eyes made his smile look like a mask. Corwin's long, manicured fingers rested upon her shoulder, and his black eyes did not leave her face. "Please join us, Journeywoman Byronia." The touch was the only affection he would give in front of others.

"Thank you, House Master Corwin." Byronia bent her head towards her uncle and the other masters in turn, speaking to the human last as she was the host. "House Master Gabena and House Master Jaren, I brought the bulls from Port Denwort. They were brought into the vault. From my observations, humans used them only as mounts, not war beasts, but they are sturdy and have no fear."

She set her notes on the table and took a sip of the offered mead. Perfectly light and refreshing on the tongue, she didn't care if it was poisoned.

"Did you see the humans work on them?" Jaren asked.

"No, House Master. The overseers rode them, then guided them to a barn, turned them off and went to play cards. I brought the tools which were kept with the beasts, though none look too specialized to my untrained eye."

"Deaths?"

"A single guard. I brought him with the beasts, but there is no doubt blood on the floor of the barn."

"Thank you, Lady Byronia," Jaren said. "The rest of the House Masters will assemble and discuss this. If you discover the inventor, please report immediately. Where are you staying?"

"The Golden Sea due to their long Guild association." She took another sip.

"Excellent. Then we look forward to your reports."

She wished to speak with her uncle but knew she was dismissed. Her cup of delicious mead was still mostly full. At least, she had been invited for tea at the safehouse.

※

Chapter 4
Port Denwort
in the Realm of Dynion

"THERE'S A THIEF TO BE EXECUTED TODAY," Edar said at breakfast. "Would you be a dear and cut down the body? I'll send a message in the morning post to the mayor."

"Is your executioner decent?" Roark asked.

"The neck will snap. He should be quite dead." Edar sighed. "It is really too bad. The man is only twenty-one. I'd like to walk in a young man's form."

"You can do that?" Roark's insides trembled. If Edar could transmutate, he must report it to Corwin.

Edar tapped his fingers upon the hearthstone. "Two necromancers have tried ... and failed. I have the history of one in my labs. Read it prudently, Roark. The other is a tale of a potion that allows the drinker to jump bodies. However, I don't have a complete recipe. But imagine, if I had a living body, we could dine at the Black Lion. Maybe I'd even find a pretty maid to dance with. It's been some time since I was with a maid."

Roark nodded, glad Edar had not considered stealing his body as an option. "When is the hanging?"

※

THE HOT AFTERNOON SUN BEAT HIS HEAD and burned his tripoint ears as Roark examined the condemned. Edar wouldn't have wanted this body; the human male was emaciated. The condemned's eyes were opened so wide that Roark could see the jaundice as the executioner tied his hands to his back and legs together. He moaned, opening his toothless mouth as the executioner put a rope around his neck.

Through gasps, Mayor Kleidmacher stated, "You have been caught stealing by our magistrate, and you have been judged guilty.

"By the laws of this Realm, you will hang till you are dead. By the laws of Port Denwort, I condemn you. May the Waters of Resurrection wash you clean."

Behind the mayor, his grandson signaled the executioner.

The crowd cheered.

Roark refused to let himself blink as he observed the last few moments of light in the man's eyes.

The executioner knocked back the lever to the gallows. The man's eyes widened as he fell. His neck broke cleanly. Feces spilled down his leg and plopped on the ground. His light disappeared.

A few street urchins scurried over and ripped off his clothing. The crowd cheered again. With nothing else to see, the spectators wandered back to their ordinary lives. It was a busy market day. Nearly every space was filled with basket weavers, pot makers, and farmers. Since the mayor's executioner gave him leave, no one minded the Fairsinge taking the corpse.

As Edar instructed, Roark wrapped him in tarred leather and tossed the man over his shoulder. The mayor's youngest guard helped him put the corpse in a wagon. Sweat coating every inch of his skin, he trudged back up the hill to Edar's cottage. He stopped to drink a tall cup of water once inside, then carried the corpse down the stairs to the basement.

Edar chopped ice which he put into a metal tray, which he slid under his metal table. He set clean cotton gauze on the ice. "We always must keep the subject cold to slow the decomposition."

Roark set the body upon the table and cut off the scraps of fabrics still hanging from his body.

"This man is thinner than I'd hoped ... so many are hungry." Edar examined the subject's blackened nailbeds and rotten teeth. "Unusable!"

With a sharp short knife, he cut out the tongue and eyeballs and dropped them into a beaker of whiskey. Edar washed the knife and made three incisions into the throat. He removed the larynx and sliced it into small pieces which he dropped into the beaker.

"Truthsayer's potion. The mayor's guard often uses it. Please move it to the north wall and bring that tray of gallon jars."

Roark did as he was bid. It was common enough practice in the Guild to loosen tongues with simple whiskey. However, perhaps being showed a jar of someone's eyes and tongue might scare truth out of some.

Edar cut open the torso.

"Is that the normal size of a human liver? The one you have seems smaller," Roark said.

"It's enlarged. A young man should be much healthier. Still, his heart, lungs, and kidneys can make decent remedies. And his manhood can still be dried for the mayor."

"Why does that happen?"

"Most likely, he was starving."

Roark thought about the rise of the slave trade, families of brigands in the forests, the elderly and children scraping out an existence. He remembered every person he'd killed over the years. *How many were stealing because they were hungry? Dear Goddess of the Resurrection, what if that happened to me?*

"What are you thinking?"

"How I don't want to be resurrected as this man."

"Nor I, my friend." Edar covered the cadaver with the wet gauze.

※

Chapter 5
Port Denwort
in the Realm of Dynion

A NOTHER LONG AND PAINFUL NIGHTMARE haunted Roark. Feeling a dagger slice open his cheek, he leapt from bed. He was alone, alive and in the relative safety of Edar's mother's room. He moved to the dressing table and gazed at his reflection in the mirror. His flesh was intact. He was still beautiful.

The sky outside his window was the pale blue of predawn. Roark's hand trembled over his saddlebags. These weeks he had learned much, but it was time to leave for a job and report to Corwin. He hoped the recipe for the Healing Blood and Truthsayer's potions would be enough.

In the kitchen, Edar hummed as he pulled bread from the oven. A bandage, a ceramic beaker of blue powder, herbs, and an empty pot and ceramic from the lab sat upon the table, but Edar didn't speak of the donation. Instead, he cut off a thick hunk of bread and placed it in front of Roark and put out a jar of quince jam. "I could cook kidneys to strengthen you?"

Kidneys and toast did not sound appetizing, but Roark would need his vigor both for his donation and travel, so he agreed. Behind him, meat sizzled as Edar dropped it into hot butter.

Edar pushed a bench to sit beside Roark. Perching on his chair, his eyes grew wide as Roark sliced open the scar on his arm and leaned so the blood could fall into the waiting cup.

The quartz shivered under Roark's shirt. It also desired the spilled blood, but Edar could never know about that.

Edar licked his lips. His milky pupils dilated. He was so focused on the blood, Roark prodded gently, "Are those kidneys going to burn?"

"No, no that wouldn't do." The lich's silk shoes squeaked across the wood floor as he hurried back to the stove.

Roark wet his finger with the blood and smeared it on the quartz while the lich's back was turned. He was finished before Edar dished the plate of kidneys and set it before him.

While Roark bled into the cup, Edar mixed the potion. He added a bit of water and smashed the blue powder and herbs into a paste which he placed in the pot.

He put the pot into the flame and watched the paste spark. The lich gently swirled the cup of blood and drizzled it with his concoction, stirring it slowly. "We must be careful to not let it clot early."

Roark bandaged his arm. "The kidneys look wonderful."

"Thank you."

As Roark ate his breakfast, Edar drank the blood potion. His carotid artery pulsed; his flesh grew flushed and pink. He licked the cup, trying to get each drop. Then his lips. He checked his chin with his hand and tasted the fallen morsel.

"You will return, Lord Roark?"

"Assuming I don't die on the battlefield."

Though Edar's skin was slowly taking on the signals of life, it sagged deeper than usual.

Roark patted his hand. "Fear not. I've spent too much time with my aunt. That's what she always says. I don't think I can bring back a whole body, but I'll bring back samples to help us with our work."

Edar smiled, and Roark noticed the smile wasn't so gruesome with fresh blood in his veins. Edar's gums had puffed and returned to a more natural pink color.

✳

Micagrav Harbor
in the Realm of Iarcia

WEAK FROM HIS DONATION, ROARK LIFTED his hand toward the sun and counted the fingers to the horizon. Jaci ensured he was on time, but the dock was empty of any Expanse-faring ships and the beach mostly deserted as well, except for seagulls and a few dwarven women collecting mussels in the distance.

Roark threw a stone into the sea, watching it skip once, and crash into a wave. He thought about his report. He learned a lonely lich can make a wonderful host. He also learned he didn't like the conflict he felt deep within his soul. However, Corwin wouldn't care about that.

The apprenticeship was a reciprocal relationship, but Edar didn't have to ask after Roark's comfort or cook kidneys and fresh bread for him. Roark thought about writing to Alana for advice on how she dealt with the conflict between the vows she made as a Fairsinge Martlet and as a Guild War Ender. That was pointless; he would worry her over a question he knew the answer to: Alana was a Martlet first and foremost.

Roark heard the soft shuffle of stones behind him. He put his hand on his knife but didn't unsheathe it as he turned.

They didn't have to let him know they were there.

He did not take his eyes off the dwarves who approached as he bowed before Kajsa Goldsvein, a lovely middle-aged dwarf-woman of fine breeding and taste. Her long blonde hair and beard were plaited neatly with a band of translucent silk which set off the delicate rosy coloring of her skin.

"We're hiring you instead of Sewryn, so you better be as good with poisons as he," Kajsa said. Behind her as always was Doriel Angrock, the widower of Kajsa's elder sister, who walked with purpose and resolve of the regular soldier that he once was. Only now, his body was incomplete and his weaponry lighter; Doriel's left forearm ended in a stump.

Though Roark had worked with them many times, it was a new experience to work alone. "I won't disappoint, my Lady-in-arms, Master Doriel." Roark inclined his head slightly in the language of the Larcian Dwarves, matching her highborn accent.

"You better not. I will kill you before I let you slander our Great Lady's name with incompetence," she replied without anger or malice in the same tongue. Roark did not doubt Kajsa's resolve. Roark's performance affected the War Ender who hired him. The jobs of any Journeyman Assassin before they earned a reputation were the most dangerous because they were the most expendable.

"Break bread with us, Roark. I want to explain the way the boulder rolls." Kajsa pulled out a bottle of mead which she poured into flagons. Doriel unwrapped boiled buns, fiddling with the cloth bag's knot with his teeth.

Their last job was the reason that Doriel suffered amputation. Did they blame him?

"Can I help?" Roark asked.

"No," Doriel grumbled. The knot loosened enough to open the bag with his other hand.

"Should I cast a circle?" Roark asked.

Doriel shook his head and held out the bag first to Kajsa and then to him. "Who will hear us? Or care. The seagulls?"

Roark took an offered bun, his mind spinning with the danger. He took a bite; it was filled with minced meat and gravy.

Unlike his own people, dwarves were patriarchal. If Doriel wanted to kill Roark, would Kajsa be able to stop him? She outranked him both by birth and in the Guild. He was a male and five years older. He didn't know which system Doriel held in more esteem. Roark still couldn't tell. If they were lovers, would one be in charge?

"Stop," Doriel punched Roark's shoulder with his remaining hand.

"Stop what?"

"By the way you are staring, you know what I speak. I'd hate to cause Lady Alana sadness if her nephew compromised Lady Kajsa's reputation on his very first job."

Heat radiated up Roark's throat to his cheeks.

"We aren't any of your business," Doriel said.

Kajsa laughed. "But, good to know we're keeping the gossip mill turning. Alana didn't tell you how the two of us came to work for the Guild?"

"Some of it." Actually, Roark knew all of it but was glad for the story. It was a filthy stereotype, but in general, dwarves didn't bother telling yarns to those they planned to kill.

Kajsa swallowed the rest of her bun in two bites and took a long sip from her flagon. "House Goldsvein's suffered both in the loss of sons and depleted coffers during the decades-long 'skirmish' for the river with the Copperbloods. But the commoners who worked the river and mines suffered most of all. Sons were taken away to fight; daughters were left to tend the land, which was made rocky by the blood of our people.

"My grandfather hoped to gain honor before we were gone in a foolish battle which escalated quickly, however, my father, in a bid to save us, called in the Guild. Without funds to pay a War Ender, the price was one of my generation. My grandfather and father thought they got a deal because I was a quarrelsome daughter."

"Now, Kajsa is the most loved of his children and the crown prince's most loved sister because Goldsvein's coffers run deep with what we send from our work." Doriel's tone was greasy with resentment towards the male side of the Goldsvein family.

"As a foot soldier, Doriel proved himself in battle and rose quickly as a leader of men. After my father was wounded, he struck a bargain with Doriel to lead his army to victory. My sister was unmarriageable without a dowry."

Kajsa glanced over at Doriel. He did not speak.

Lowest Realm, he is going to kill me, Roark thought.

Remain calm, the quartz whispered.

"For his part, Doriel was a happy and faithful husband until Kalota died in childbirth. My niece lived two days after my sister. He found no friendship or even sympathy from any quarter of my House. My mother was so grief-stricken. My brothers thought he was an upstart. Father sent him away.

"Doriel plotted revenge from a small mountain fort where stories of his bravery held the hearts of men." She paused again to allow her brother-in-law to continue his story.

"Alana and Kajsa came for me before I stupidly carried out my plans, which would've restarted the war. We made a bargain. If I allowed Larcia to heal, Lady Alana would call in a favor for my situation. I was an apprentice for a year to learn Guild ways, then I could be a man-at-arms of any War Ender I chose. I owe the great lady much, but I owe her nephew nothing."

Doriel's coarse words were directed towards him, but there was no malice.

"I'm sorry about your hand. We wouldn't have been able to cross the fairy-fire without your sacrifice."

"I got paid for my sacrifice, and I got another hand still strong enough to take you." Doriel threw another punch to Roark's shoulder; this one landed hard enough to hurt. Roark couldn't tell if Doriel didn't blame him. Or if Doriel blamed him and would hurt him someday, though his Lady-in-Arms would be using Roark for the job so he couldn't hurt him now.

"Doriel's been training with throwing hatchets and several lighter swords for the months we've been parted," Kajsa said. "It's a different style of fighting, but Seweryn's been a good teacher."

"Sarding light blades bend too easily," Doriel grumbled. "If I had puny arms like yours, I would wield it better."

Though Roark would never be a War Ender, his time with Alana taught him that War Enders plan for all contingencies. Even getting their assassin used to their brother-in-law. Or perhaps getting their brother-in-law used to a new assassin. Everything was planned. Kajsa and Doriel's friendship went deep, and they were stronger together, even with the loss of a sword hand.

It wouldn't be a good life if I lived forever without companionship. Roark decided once he got a bit closer to success, he would think about how to ask them. Kajsa might be up for it, but Doriel seemed too dour for eternal life, especially without a whole body. *But if transmutation is real, maybe ...*

※

Dear Byronia,
I heard you're back in Port Denwort. I believe I discovered the last missing boy from our list. Rataen was bought by a spice merchant named Nelson Grayhook in Port Welliver.

May the Goddess watch over your journey, Alana

Chapter 6
Port Denwort
in the Realm of Dynion

BYRONIA TWISTED THE PARCHMENT INTO A tight scroll and slipped it into her pocket. Port Welliver was a few days ride, but first, she must discover who created the bulls and for what purpose.

She dressed in the modest gown of a human peasant and cloaked her blond braids with a veil as was common in married women in Port Denwort, which would also cover her ears. She carefully softened her cheeks with rouge and darkened under her eyes with ash.

Slouching, she moved slowly down the docks and entered Salty Eel Tavern—a favorite among the overseers. The door's rusty metal hinges announced her arrival. The innkeeper nodded her way, but the tavern inhabitants scarcely took notice. The peppery smell of burnt leaf tickled her nose. A few rentboys and girls lingered about and tried to catch her eye, but she kept her gaze downcast.

Most patrons drank a dark beer and had a bowl of pottage—including one of the plantation overseers. She ordered the same, paid in copper, and found a quiet table in the corner. The day's pottage was a loose broth of carrots, chicken—maybe squab. A bit bland on the tongue, but it was warm and welcoming in her stomach.

Two Larcian sailors sat in the corner, but otherwise, most of the clientele looked to be human of the poorer merchant class, sailors, rentboys and girls.

The hinges screamed again as a group filed in wearing long brightly-colored robes of vibrant purple, emerald, or sapphire, which seemed to shimmer in the candlelight. Their laughter rang out in the dim tavern. Whoever these people were, they seemed to enjoy a jolly time. The innkeeper quickly brought them three carafes of wine, and the rentboys and girls approached their table.

The overseer scowled their way and hurried out. Byronia made note of it.

At first glance, the beings looked to be large specimens of humans, but something was off about them. She sensed they weren't altogether natural.

They were the basic shape of all the intelligent species of the Realms, and Byronia quickly sketched the party, making notes of every commonality and difference between them and the other sentients of the Seven Realms. She could not tell if they were male, female or another gender. They moved and spoke thoughtfully—more like a Telchine or a gnome compared to fast-talking humans and elfkin. Their stature was slightly larger than most humans, but not overtly so. They were hairier than most dwarves, but their golden locks were coiffed in rich curls, their mustaches braided into their beards in a different weave than was common in the dwarf-inhabited Larcia. Their skin looked pale, as if the sun never touched them, and had an under hue of lavender—though that might be a reflection of their shimmering clothing and cosmetics. The group had human-shaped ears. However, when one turned in her direction, Byronia was stricken by the eyes: glassy orbs filled with an opalescent violet liquid and a single enlarged purple iris.

She turned the page in her book and ordered another beer.

The hinges screamed again. The overseer and six other human males from the plantation entered the tavern. Though she didn't think they would recognize her as "the angel who saved the elfkin slaves," Byronia slid closer to the wall.

"Where're our oxen?"

"Whatever in the world are you talking about?" the one in embroidered golden robes asked. The being's hair swirled around hir like it had a mind of its own. Once Byronia wrote that note, she almost crossed it out. That's stupid. But not as stupid as not having an open mind, she recited from one of Corwin's old lessons.

"Our oxen. They disappeared." The human man hit the wooden table which shuddered under his punch. "And we're missing a guard."

"Then I would think you should file a complaint with the magistrate."

"Don't give us that."

"Perhaps your missing man took them," the being said.

The overseer drew a knife.

The individual in the golden robe screamed. The entire party, along with the rentboys and girls, drew back.

From the bar, the innkeeper lifted a cleaver. "You want a drink, or you want to be moving along."

The entire tavern held their breath and waited to see what would happen.

The human overseers left, huffing, slamming the wooden door behind them hard enough that it bounced on its squeaky hinges.

The beings' party went on with nervous laughter and twittering as the innkeeper brought another carafe.

Byronia noticed a rash covering a rentboy's bare arms. *Had it been there when she arrived?* She couldn't remember.

Their party went on long into the night. They seemed to be a merry sort of folk, laughing and singing songs which Byronia did not know.

She was glad; it gave her plenty of time to draw and make notes of her observations. She hoped her uncle and the other House Masters would be pleased.

*

Port Welliver
in the Realm of Dynion

ESTABLISHED ON A PENINSULA, PORT Welliver was home to a small human population, but like many of the ports on the North Sea, the elfkin and other species of the Seven Realms were not unknown. Byronia would not blend in with the populous, but she wouldn't stand out either. From the outside, it looked like a quaint and cozy fishing village, but as she approached the gate, it was easy to spot half-rotten rooftops. Vines had taken over some structures, coating them in green. These vines made ladders for the rats and other vermin. No one, not even the poorest, came near the road for alms.

Around the wall, townspeople scratched at their blemish- and welt-covered skin. They stood in long lines towards the gate where one man and two women were armed and on their feet. They handed metal bowls of soup to those who came.

"Hey, ho," Byronia called.

"Milady, ride from here. Come no closer," the older of the two women said.

"What is this sickness?" she asked.

"Something the sailors brought."

"Which sailors?"

"Does it matter?"

"I supposed not. Have you seen any strange folk?" she asked.

"Well, you," the older woman said.

"Welliver knows the elfkin. And I know a remedy man in Denwort. I could beg for help."

"We know we will die. Our healthy children have already abandoned us. We tend to those who come to the gate. The rest starve in their beds."

"I seek an elfkin slave boy of twelve. His name is Rataen. He would've been brought here by a merchant Grayhook. I wish to buy him back."

"Grayhook's dead as are his two servants. We already burnt the bodies," the man called. "One was an elf boy, never knew his name."

She thanked them for the information.

Byronia rode until she made it upstream several miles away. She constructed a large fire and boiled all of her clothing and gear. She washed Joy and bathed in the creek, then smeared lanoline on them both.

Everything she had on her person was made clean before she wrote the bad news to Alana and sent the information on to The Guild Masters.

❄

Chapter 7
Outskirts of City of Cheripol
in the Realm of Cannik

U NDER THE WATCHFUL EYES OF ANCIENT stone Water Gods of the Vodnik long covered with green moss, Roark awaited Kajsa's signal. However, in the filtered light of the dense canopy of spruce and moss, he could not find peace. Mountain sparrows swooped at insects and fluttered away with their kills. This was to be a poisoning with a complicated delivery. The carved cave shelter was simply furnished with a tiny fireplace and a few cots, but Roark found it claustrophobic to be inside for too long. It was better to sit in the shade of the trees and be close to all the living things of the forests.

It would be a few days before his part would be needed, but he kept his eyes on the fort in the river valley below in case something went wrong. Stacked river rock and hardwood beams held the fort's wooden structure which was topped with the Vodnik's customary limestone dome. Roark couldn't quite make out how many were inside through the dirty, leaded windows, but several commoners were outside the fort working. It would be easy to destroy the fort and all within with limited Guild explosives, but that wasn't the job—especially now that Kajsa, Doriel and their entourage were inside.

Perhaps, he thought, *I'm worried because Alana can no longer step in if I sard up.* His aim and timing needed to be perfect, but he did not fear for his aim and timing. He never felt like this before. Roark killed in protection of others or for the good of the Fairsinge people. Collateral damage never sat well with him. He'd never slaughtered an innocent and had no wish to start. That's why he ended his apprenticeship before he became a War Ender. An assassin's marks were never innocent.

Roark wandered to the edge of headlands and beheld an overview of the situation. He stood upon a narrow channel of nearly vertical rock as he gazed northwards and memorized the scene. How much the dossier told him, and yet how little. His mark was a Vodnik nobleman who craved war and soon would be survived by a wife and three children. The wife would be named Regent, and Kajsa's silver tongue would smooth over his people's tattered feelings. One death instead of many. From his perch, Roark witnessed his mark leave the fort astride his horse with two guards riding behind him. The Vodnik were a handsome people, their skin colored by the high percentage of copper in their blood in every shade of green from the palest sea mist to the darkest olive. Their hair, which started white and darkened to black as they aged, was worn in large braids entwined with metal ribbons which denoted their principality and rank. His mark had deep green skin and gray hair intertwined with gold and silver.

He had not received the signal to kill him yet. Roark opened his mind and felt the bloodlust in their veins. He understood Kajsa's choice. Duplicity was a risk when hiring the Guild.

He couldn't stop them, but he knew that around the bend, an elderly Vodnik woman washed laundry in the stream. Her black braids had no ornamentation.

Roark wished he could signal the laundress in some way and tell her to run before the mark saw her. He yearned to come up with a plan. His mind went blank. *Why hadn't I studied strategy with more dedication?*

Moments later, it was too late. The men laughed as soon as they discovered her.

Roark would enjoy killing him; his hands itched to do it. Instead, he observed the nobleman order one of his soldiers to trample the old woman.

The soldier did so. They rode away cheering.

Knowing he must not be seen either by his mark or Kajsa's team, Roark crept to the dying woman. Tawny-colored blood dripped out of her mouth and frothed as it hit the ground. Roark had seen many Vodnik die over the years; still, he might learn something before her body liquefied.

"Why am I worthy of life and this woman worthy of death?" Roark whispered. "I spit on random chance."

She moaned and gestured towards him, before spitting more blood.

In Vodnici, Roark whispered, "I can offer you a quick death."

She might have nodded or shuddered in pain.

He cut her throat.

Within seconds, her green eyes softened to the color of milk. He cut off her hand and opened her chest. He allowed one of his older blades to chop through her ribs and removed the heart. He let the tawny blood drip into a vial before covering it with a tarred sack.

Feeling inspired, Roark crossed to the rocky embankment staying low to the ground. He took a sample of the local river water to compare it to the coppery blood of the Vodnik in Edar's lab.

He labeled each specimen, wrapped them in an old undertunic, and placed them in a tarred sack which he stuffed deep into his knapsack. He wanted to gather more, but carrying several bundles of body parts might be noticed.

※

F OUR DAYS LATER, KAJSA'S CROW FLEW IN the air and landed inside the cave shelter. It was time.

He hurried back to the headlands and placed himself in the channel. Below, outside the fort, the area filled with Vodnici citizenry and a small contingent of dwarves. Doriel wore a crown and indigo velvets; Kajsa dressed as his queen. Several "counselors" were beside them.

Roark aimed his sling armed with a capsule containing a fly coated in a fast-acting poison for the mark's mouth as he orated about the coming war with the humans who were creating new illegal technology.

Once Roark captured the rhythm of his mark's words, he took his shot.

The nobleman choked as the capsule flew into his mouth.

He coughed and spit out what looked like a simple fly with a laugh. He opened his mouth to speak again, then grasped upon his throat. He coughed. Clutching at his neck, the mark's throat swelled, cutting off his primary breathing route. Guards surrounded him and carried him out of the room away.

Kajsa stood beside the nobleman's wife. She whispered into her ear and handed her a parchment. The wife gripped the paper so tightly it creased. Then she took her husband's place and spoke.

Roark couldn't stay to hear what she had to say though he understood it was a quick speech about not giving into fear and hate, and prioritizing her citizenry's needs over a war with humans. One death had blocked the war for a decade, maybe longer.

He hurried down the tree line, running parallel to the open valley until dawn, and crossed backcountry to the unseen place deep within the Earth where he would meet Kajsa, who would bring him on to the Guild House.

✳

Chapter 8
Port Denwort
in the Realm of Dynion

BYRONIA FOLLOWED THE FINELY DRESSED being who drunkenly moved down long, uneven steps. Uncle and other Guild House Masters believed this might be an Eighth Realm creature though they had not confirmed that. It had been several centuries since any new intelligent people had been discovered, and no one wanted to spread rumors though everyone at the Salty Eel and Golden Sea were talking about the strangers.

The sound of footfalls disappeared; she slowed, straining to hear them. Darkness was all around her; the only light was a single torch from a window in the distance. A baby or young child screamed. She scanned the horizon and spotted a child in the distance, its distorted limbs circled towards the sky. As she grew closer, she observed he was a boy. His mouth hung open as if his jaw was broken. Lesions surrounded by a rash encircled his flushed cheeks. He made one more wheezing cry and died.

Byronia inspected the body. *The disease in Port Welliver is here!*

Hoping she hadn't fated her ivory skin to pox, she bundled the child into a sack and hurried to Edar's cottage.

"My lady, what can I do for you?"

"I need to speak with you and Roark."

"Roark left for a job."

Byronia frowned. "Then please listen. Port Welliver is gone. They're burning the bodies. And I found an abandoned child covered in lesions. I brought you the body so you could see the rash."

"A rash? I've treated several rashes of late, but you say Port Welliver is burning bodies?"

"Yes. There were only a few healthy adults when I was there."

"Come to my laboratory, if you would."

She unbundled the child's corpse on the centermost table as Edar lit his lanterns. Other than the pile of body parts in the corner, the laboratory reminded her of a Guild surgeon's examination theater. Edgar grabbed some heavy paper cards which had spots marked in ink. He found the pattern and nodded.

"Yes, the rash is in the familiar configuration, but I've not seen these lesions before."

He created a new card. Under the drawing of the rash, he wrote: **Phase 2?**

"Bring me that stacked lens. Be gentle with it."

She did so.

"This rash is strange."

"How so?"

"It's almost as if the pore was punctured by needles instead of something raising the skin from underneath. Take a look."

The mark was raised like a flat plateau with a small hole in the center. "It almost looks like hives from a bee sting."

"Indeed." Edar labeled a specimen jar and poured alcohol over the corpse.

"I must report this," Byronia said.

Edar placed his hand on Byronia's hand. "And my

activities?"

"You have provided me with protection on occasion. I simply do not see anything out of the ordinary here. Can I have the corpse?"

"Of course. After you finish handling it, wash up good. I'd hate for your pretty face to waste away."

"I wouldn't want that either," Byronia said.

※

Chapter 9
Guild House of Olentir
in the Realm of Fairhdel

ROARK'S OLD FEAR OF THE WRINKLED HOUSE Master Corwin set in immediately upon entering the darkened chambers. He almost kneeled but remembered he was a Journeyman and bowed.

He brought forth the recipes and set them upon Corwin's counting table. "This is the potion that made Alana young." He repeated what Edar told him about the donor.

"When was the last time you donated blood?"

"Before I left for Kajsa's job. Candlewick gave me kidneys to strengthen me."

"How often does your master take your blood?"

"This is the first time. He wants to look alive, not young. His ultimate goal is to transmutate into another body."

"Interesting. I have something for you."

Corwin led Roark through the darkness until he came to a case of books.

"Alana informed me that Daena worked with Edar when they were young." Corwin opened the case and removed a tome which he put on a wooden podium. "What do you see?"

Roark skimmed what Daena called *The Great Work*. Halfway through the book, her light, near-calligraphic hand changed abruptly to a blocky printed style. The last entry in her original hand spoke of her trying a spell of transmutation. He hoped that was what the House Master wanted him to see.

"Did you know Daena was nearly a century old when you met her?"

"She looked and sounded to be a woman in her prime."

"Indeed."

"And you believe it was a transmutation?"

"Yes. Most likely, she took one of the slaves from House Josel. No doubt the Empress didn't even notice. And her lord consort wouldn't have cared."

The horror settled within Roark's chest. "We took the quartz."

"So you did."

He knew the answer but wanted it to be spoken and made real. "How did you get this book?"

"I had Daena killed." Corwin handed Roark a newer tome. "I copied it exactly, so Candlewick can't recognize Daena's writing. Take this to your master."

"But why?"

"The Guild must know if the transmutation spell works as written. This is not a ritual for the faint-hearted."

It wasn't. In fact, it was more violent than the spell which Edar had in his library.

"But House Master, give me more time, please."

Corwin's smile disappeared. He slapped the side of Roark's head. "Show your master this spell. If he is as good as you think, he won't do it. If he is not, then he will. Now, I would like to sample your blood before you go, and I want you to see into your, our, people's future."

Roark lay on the velvet divan as Corwin reopened the cut on his arm, carefully measuring out the blood.

"Go eight years from this day. Stay at the Guild House."

Closing his eyes, Roark thought of his future. Eight years from his moment, he would be twenty-six summers with two years left on his Guild Journey. Roark's soul left his corporeal form, and he drifted into a misty reverie. Corwin's voice resounded all around him to assist him in finding his way. He walked through the dark mists until he found himself outside the Guild House on the eastern side between the fenced paddock where several Guild warhorses grazed with a few sheep, and a row of Guild Worker's apartments.

In the uppermost floor to the east, shutters were thrown open. Green smoke poured out the open window. Kian coughed and pressed an auburn-haired tot to his chest tightly.

"No. No. I cold!" She fretted, shaking her head. Kian wrapped her in his jacket but didn't leave the window until the air cleared. "Stop moving. You'll fall."

Though he didn't have his brother's bulk, at twenty-one, the scrawny kid had grown into a wiry man whose eyes held boundless intelligence. There were too many signs of wealth for him to be a Guild Workman: his clothes were finely woven, his reddish-blond curls shined, and his beard was trimmed close to his face. Under his beard, a few blemishes marred an otherwise healthy complexion.

Roark's spirit floated to the window. Kian carried his child inside, set her into an improvised wooden fence where a thick wool blanket, a few blocks and a doll spread around her. She babbled to herself, or possibly to Kian. He sat in a leather chair, leaning over a great desk and made notes in his manuscript. Roark liked the quizzical smile the man wore. He briefly wondered how he would feel in Kian's arms.

That's still Eohan's little brother. And right now, he's thirteen.

Kian went to the exam table. Using the flat blade,

he scraped the smoldering rat bits into a metal bucket. "Why didn't that work?" he muttered to himself.

Roark glanced at Kian's desk where several manuscripts and scrolls lay. Fingerprints and half-scribbled notes surrounded a drawing of the Water of the Resurrection. Below, in his Aunt Alana's three-step code, was a recipe entitled: Living Death.

The child raised her arms to Roark. "Pick me up! Pick me up! Lord Fata!" She waved her tiny chubby fingers towards the ether. Though Roark knew he could not be hurt, he backed into the wall.

"Your lord father isn't here, and I'm busy, dearling, but if you're good, you can have honey toast when I'm done," Kian said without turning toward her.

"Honey toast," she repeated. Following Roark's movements with Byronia's deep-as-the-Expanse sapphire eyes. "You a ghost? Boo!" The child hid behind her fence and popped her head up. "Boo!"

"Would you focus?" Corwin's voice echoed across time.

Roark noticed several dried corpses stacked in the corner. Each one's body covered in welts.

"A new disease is spreading," Corwin said.

The child smiled and laughed. Her laugh ended in a little sigh. There it was: Byronia was this child's mother, but that was his auntie's laugh, his sister's smile. Oh, dear Goddess, Roark would never have chosen this. A War Ender promoted to House Master would always have a backup plan. *This child was Corwin's backup plan. Did that mean House Silba was fated to fall? Or House Eyreid.*

When Roark didn't respond to her, the girl made a shriek-worthy of a dragon. A white-pawed black cat carrying a rat popped into the room, dropped the rat at Kian's feet, and jumped over the fence and rubbed its head upon her.

"Would you stop playing with that child and come back? You aren't my only appointment today."

Roark wandered through the mists and back in time to where Corwin was leering over him.

"You saw the future," Corwin said.

"Kian with a child. My child."

"I prefer to think of Alana the Second as Byronia's child. A noble child whose curse is so strong that she will rewrite our legends."

"And if I choose not to?"

Corwin smacked his ear. "Then I will look to other Great Houses for the continuation of the Curse because our future grows short. However, I was trying to show you a possible epidemic. Byronia found it in Port Denwort. Keep those eyes and ears open."

※

CAREFUL HIS WRIST WAS BOUND TIGHTLY and no longer bleeding, Roark moved through the rectory. He scanned for familiar faces which dotted the crowd. He found Alana, Eohan, and Kian at a table. The wrinkles on Alana's face seemed more profound and more silver-lined than faded auburn. He hoped she cared for herself as well as she cared for her apprentices. She deserved his blood potions more than Corwin.

Roark felt for Kian whose face had sprouted acne. Thirteen summers were rarely kind and especially awful when one had an elder brother of twenty to compare to. Eohan's shoulders took the space of two ordinary Fairsinge men; he sat straight and tall. Still, Roark knew that one day Kian would be a grown man and handsome in his own way. He had foreseen it.

He waved and hurried over. Eohan stood and crossed the room. Roark clasped Eohan's muscular forearm in greeting.

"Nalla and I are meeting later. Would you like a drink with us, Lord Roark?"

Roark didn't like his title on his friend's lips. It made him more distant somehow. "I wouldn't be imposing?"

"Not for the drinking part."

"Sure. I'll be heading back to Dynion soon, but I hoped to see you and my aunt."

Eohan frowned at the mention of a Realm—always such a rule follower.

"Did my aunt tell you what I've been doing?" Roark asked, glancing over at her.

"Of course not."

Roark lowered his voice. "Candlewick."

Eohan's face twisted into a pained frown as his hands curled into fists which he rubbed along the seams of his pants.

"I don't want to hurt you—or Kian—but the Guild must know what Edar is doing and if he has any illegal tech. I didn't want you to hear of it from someone else," Roark said quickly. "Can I still stay for the drink?"

"Yes, and I understand." Eohan picked a callus from his hand. "I probably won't tell Kian. He isn't doing well. But yes, stay. I know we don't get to pick our jobs, especially at the beginning of a journey."

"What's wrong with Kian?"

Eohan's eyes filled with gratitude. Roark didn't like that either.

"He sasses our Lady; questions everything we do. He snaps at Pa whenever we're here. He never listens to me. It was so bad on our last job, Lord Seweryn took him aside. Kian calmed for a few days, but once the lord left, it started again. Kian won't talk to me; when I question him, he gets angrier."

"Alana would say we were all thirteen once."

Eohan met his eyes. "That's what she does say. She never loses her temper."

"Is Kian keeping up his knife work?"

"Indeed. Still can't hit a target blindfolded at thirty paces though, but his fast draw is impressive."

As they came back to the table, he noted Alana and Eohan's cups held spring water. Kian's addiction might never end. Perhaps that's the source of Eohan's worry; perhaps Roark should tell him about the vision.

"You look pale. Have something to eat," Alana said. She waited for him to lean down to her before she kissed his cheek.

"Auntie, you saw Byrony's future?"

"I went into her future on her first steps as I did with you."

"What did you see?"

"A child who will fall into madness if her father does not care for her. Corwin claims she will be the greatest War Ender to ever wander the Realms. He will go to great lengths to ensure that one survives. He has been sweeter since he saw the vision."

"I don't want to be a father."

"I suppose if you don't want to be a father, you won't be."

He wanted to tell her where he had been, what he had learned but didn't dare with Kian there. He leaned next to her and whispered, "I gave Corwin a sample. I could ..."

"I can't live forever and don't fear death or weakness. My path is clear; I must get these young men taught before the future catches up to us."

Looking down at his dinner, his back hunched, Kian snapped, "You don't need to protect me, Roark."

"Lord Roark," his brother said.

"Fine. Lord Roark, I've known where you've been."

"I told you not to eavesdrop," Eohan said.

"I wasn't. You were across the room." Kian snapped. "But I knew the taste of the potion, and now he's offering his dear auntie more."

"I just don't want to hurt you."

"I'm in the Guild; no one can hurt me." Kian's voice was acid.

Thinking about the vision. "Aunt, how do you know your direction? I got lost in visions. And I was in the Guild House."

"Practice."

"You're still maddening," Roark said.

"As you often told me, but that doesn't mean you don't need practice, dearling," Alana said.

"Lady Alana, my mother sends her regard and an invitation." A pretty Daosith deckhand, Nalla, approached the table, inclined her head towards his aunt who stood and hugged the young woman. After their greeting, Nalla slipped behind Eohan and wrapped her brown arms around his neck. Her golden lips kissed the top of his dark curls. A surge of jealousy roared through Roark's chest—not over Nalla—but the fellowship he missed. Maybe necromancy was a mistake. He was bringing a dangerous spell Edar couldn't resist? To help Corwin learn what is possible?

"Kian, let us go and leave Eohan and Roark to their pleasures."

"Why can't I stay?"

"When you're his age, you will have the same freedoms and responsibilities as your brother."

Kian seethed, but ignoring the boy, Alana drew Nalla aside. Roark knew her question before she asked it. "You have protection, don't you?"

Eohan blushed.

"Yes, Lady Alana. Thank you for your concern," Nalla said.

"Good. Then I'll see you, Eohan, at dawn in the

stables."

Eohan kept his eyes on his cup. "Yes, my lady."

"Be well, my dear nephew." Alana kissed Roark's cheek and left with Kian.

"Why does your aunt insist on talking about lambsheads with Kian right there?" Eohan complained as the steward brought flagons of mead. "Kian will mention it to Pa. And Pa will carp about how Lady Alana isn't concerned with my morals. That we ought to get married."

Roark always knew which way the road turned, but since he began his journey, he felt lost. Alana spoke openly about everything she deemed essential for an apprentice to know and until his pa became a Guild baker, Eohan didn't seem to mind. "I'm sorry about my aunt." He hoped that was enough.

"No skin off my nose," Nalla said, but her voice was sad. "Lady Alana is no worse about such things than my mother. Before I disembarked, she handed me a box and said she expected me to be deckboss before I'm a grandmother." A tear rolled down her cheek which she brushed away. "Lillia's passed."

"Oh goddess," Eohan whispered.

Lillia was the venerable Guild Steward of *The Muirchlaimhte* who cared for their needs. She had always been kind and encouraging to them, but moreover was a grandmother figure to Nalla who had grown up on the ship.

Eohan drew her hands in his. "I'm sorry, my heart. May the Waters of Resurrection bring her soul to the highest station."

That epitaph rang hollow to Roark, but he did not speak. He fumbled to find a handkerchief and give it to Nalla. "What happened?"

"Mother already made her report to the Guild, but we ought to go to the garden. Loose lips you know ... "

"I rented a cell for the night," Roark said.

"Even better."

They carried their mead to Roark's small private chamber. It was empty except his gear in the locked trunk and the large bed in the center of the room. The three sat on the bed. Nalla rested her hands in her lap as she spoke.

"We saw a ship floundering in the waves of the Expanse. We pulled alongside to offer assistance. And Gnomes shot crossbow bolts at us. They had terrible aim, the only one of us hurt was Idas."

Roark nodded.

"We took their ship within minutes. Eventually, Mother spoke to their captain. They attacked us because a slave ship had attacked them. They didn't know if they could trust us with their ship so badly damaged."

Eohan nodded.

"Here's where it gets strange. The Gnomes had taken one prisoner, a Fairsinge slaver. The slaves revolted while his crew attacked the Gnomes. His crewmates are most likely dead. We took him off their hands with Guild payment."

Roark wished he could be surprised that it was one of his people who was behind the atrocity, but he wasn't. No Realm was safe anymore, and no people had the moral ground.

"Our prisoner said his ship attacked the Gnomes because they were attacked by another ship of large hairy humans who 'rescued' all the humans and Vodnik crew and slaves. They left the dwarves and Telchine.

"But the slaver was suffering from a rash. He was sick. And it spread to Lillia who cared for him during the journey. I know she was an old woman, but she was in fair health."

Eohan drew Nalla closer to him. "She died from the sickness?"

Nalla shook her head. "She bled to death while in a bath. It looked like she cut open her left ankle. That was where most of the rash was localized."

"When Mother reported to Corwin, he told me I'd see you, Roark, and I must tell you. And you ought to tell your contact in Denwort."

"Should we tell Alana?" Eohan asked.

"Captain will tell her," Nalla and Roark said together. Speaking the same thought would have customarily made Nalla laugh, but not when she was mourning her friend's death.

"What will happen to the slaver?" Eohan asked.

"He'll face Guild justice for attacking a Gnome Merchant Ship. Why doesn't that make me feel any better?"

"I don't think anything will." Eohan wiped the tears from Nalla's eyes. "I was horrified when my mother died, and Lillia was as good as any mother to you and us. I still remember the first time we met ... "

The quartz whispered, *Taste the joy of life now, but all entities will walk The Long Road unless you stop this.*

Watching Eohan gently comfort his paramour with stories of Lillia's kindness, Roark bet if he could give them the chance to love forever, they would take him up on it.

❄

Chapter 10
Port Denwort
in the Realm of Dynion

ON THE JOURNEY BACK TO PORT DENWORT, Roark studied *The Great Work* carefully. The spells Daena had tried upon herself crossed the border into madness. Several would have caused severe physical trauma.

Against the quartz's advisement, Roark decided he would tell Edar everything. He would tell him about the quartz, the Guild's interest in his work, even that the Guild killed Daena.

Only with that knowledge could Edar decide if he still wanted Roark to learn from him. Then Roark would show him the things he'd brought: the Vodnik blood, river water, heart and transmutation spell. If Edar dismissed him, he could start researching his own Great Work alone.

Roark entered the cottage's front garden, the front door had a sign that read, "Ring Bell for Service."

Edar must be in the basement, Roark thought and turned the key. The ground floor was empty as expected. He put his gear in his room and brought the samples with him to the cellar.

"Roark?" Edar called expectedly.

"Yes, I'm here and I ... "

However, Edar interrupted him, rambling about

Byronia's visit and a new rash on a corpse. "We must keep our eyes on our patients. As soon as it spreads from the first whore, they will be coming, mark my words."

"But Edar, we must speak."

"Roark, my lad, whatever you brought can wait. This might not. Port Welliver has been burned to the ground." Edar mixed lanoline with quicksilver.

"But," Roark said.

Edar slammed his mortar and pestle on his work table. "Enough. In this, I am the master. We must find a remedy for this new disease and begin to test them before the disease sweeps through Port Denwort. Now, be a good lad, put those things away, and crush some wormwood."

The quartz shivered. Wait. The vision of rash-covered corpses flew into his memory. Roark tried another tact. "A sailor friend of mine saw the rash."

Edar stared at him. "And did you make love to this man?"

"No. She's not a man."

"Good because I don't know how it spreads yet. Where's that crushed wormwood?"

The quartz shivered again. Roark did as he was bid.

※

Chapter 11
Port Denwort
in the Realm of Dynion

T HE SETTING SUN WAS COVERED BY DARK clouds and snowflakes fluttered to the ground, but Byronia didn't think it was cold enough to stick. Waves crashed against the shore, spraying the docks with icy water. The smaller ships were huddled together. The larger ships moved out to sea or back into the Expanse. She didn't want to go back to the Salty Eel Tavern, but she needed to keep her eyes open.

Byronia observed one of the finely-dressed being's hair sliding around a rentboy like tentacles until the tips pressed themselves into his flesh. The boy became withered, older somehow. Once the being released him, the boy yawned and fell back against a wall. His flesh reddened with small pimples left where the hair had touched him.

Uncle said it might be a new species, perhaps from an Eighth yet unexplored Realm.

Byronia sensed eyes upon her. She glanced over her shoulder and caught the one in the blue and gold robes staring at her. She turned the page in her journal and scribbled down a list in code.

He/She/Sie/Ze/It? came to her table. The one was larger than her, as it was larger than most humans, so size did not dictate its masculinity; as her habit, Byronia settled upon she.

The one's eyes were veiled by a long, tangled mane

of golden locks, but she wore no beard, not even fuzz, though it seemed as if she had some thick body hair. Even in the loose azure robes, Byronia could see brawny shoulders and trim waist. Her golden hair swayed against the movements of her body.

The one leaned towards Byronia; her voice spoke each word in a soft musical cadence as if she sang her words. "I've seen you the past few nights, sitting in the corner, scribbling in that book. What are you writing?"

"I'm a poet," Byronia lied. She didn't like being seated while the taller being stood over her. It gave the taller too much of a tactical advantage.

"Can I see your poems?"

Byronia rose to her feet and slipped her journal into her waist bag. "I have nothing on me ready to recite, excuse me."

"Can I buy you an ale?" She placed a hairy-knuckled hand upon Byronia's forearm. Her golden locks floated towards her and swept her face. The being frowned.

"No." Without putting power into her defense, Byronia turned quickly, forcing her to break her grasp. She went to the bar, hoping her skin wasn't reddened and pockmarked.

The being followed her. "I'd really like to see one of your poems."

"I said no. What does a woman have to do to have some peace?"

"The woman said, no." the bartender said. "Plenty of rentgirls if that's what you fancy."

"Don't you have anything better to do?" The being threw a few silvers on the bar. The bartender pocketed them and went to look on other customers.

There were too many unknown factors in the tavern; Byronia had to escape. She wouldn't let down her cover in Port Denwort. She hurried out the door to the abandoned market. With a quick pace, she crossed the empty square. The wind whipped her braids and carried her veil down the street. She hoped her ears weren't showing. The flurries had not let up, and mists rested between the buildings.

Byronia dashed down the alley. She paused as she hit the next road and looked back. The being didn't run. She didn't seem to believe she had to. Perhaps those enlarged violet irises gave the beings excellent night vision.

She quickly contemplated her options. She could go back to the Golden Sea and get Guild help, but she didn't know that many human Guild members. If it went badly, she didn't want to lead the being to where she slept.

She could hide in the mists.

She could go to the mayor. Alana had told her before that he loved the nobleborn elfkin.

She could go to Edar … and Roark, if he had returned.

If she drove the one to Edar, she'd have to kill her. At least, he'd dispose of the body for her. They might even be able to tell me the species of this one.

Ensuring she caught sight of her again, Byronia crossed the street. Her pursuer was still behind her. She circled the block and headed for Edar's cottage.

The windows were dark. Byronia knocked on the door, suddenly realizing she hadn't considered Edar might not be home.

She glanced over her shoulder again. The being was looking right at her back and approached.

She pounded on the door.

From inside, Roark called, "I'm coming!" She was glad now she had someone to help her kill the being.

Rubbing sleep from his eyes, Roark opened the small window in the door. "Byrony." He opened the door.

"Don't close it. I brought you a subject."

Roark looked over her shoulder. "Will he be missed?"

"Unknown." Byronia noticed that Roark called the being a he. Maybe she was a he.

"What's all this now?" Edar said. "Lady Byronia, do you know the hour?"

"I'm in need. And I have information for all of us."

"Then come in, come in, lady."

The golden-haired being stood at Edar's gate as if deciding whether or not to come in.

Byronia stepped back to the open door ensuring she could be seen.

"Hey, ho ... I'd still like to see those poems. Maybe you have something to recite in there."

Byronia backed into the cottage.

"Now that's a body," Edar whispered from behind her.

Roark sighed. "He better not be missed."

＊

AS SOON AS THE ONE WAS THROUGH THE door, Roark grabbed him from behind and twisted his arm to his back. "My friend doesn't seem to enjoy your advances."

Without a word, the big hairy human turned and shoved him to the ground. He grabbed Byronia and tried to rip the bag from her waist. She gave him an uppercut on the chin, but he was seemingly unfazed. He growled, tore the bag away from her, and turned back towards the door.

Byronia jumped on his back and pummeled him with a dagger's pommel. He cried out in a high musical soprano.

With the hope that his vital organs should be

where most humans were on the body, Roark stabbed him in the side. Surprised by the lack of blood, Roark withdrew the knife and stuck again.

The being screamed again. Byronia quickly bound his hands behind his back and shoved a rag in his mouth. His hair seemed to have a life of its own. As a braid whistled through the wind and cracked through the air, Roark jumped back before the lash landed. The man jumped to his feet and tried to retreat.

Roark tackled him. The golden hair reached back for Roark's face. Byronia got a rope on his feet. "You alright?" she asked still holding his struggling legs.

"Yes, let's get him downstairs."

Together, they lifted the larger being, Roark at the feet and Byronia at the shoulders. They made it two steps when the golden locks wrapped around Byronia's wrists and squeezed.

She screamed as it cut off the circulation to her hands.

Edar rushed forward with a kitchen knife. He sawed through the hair holding Byronia. The being howled as if it hurt him as the hair fell away from her bruised flesh.

Edar screamed as a braid grabbed him. A thick twisting lock cut into his skin, opening a lesion. He raced past Roark to one of his lamps. He placed his wrist over his lamp and burned the strands.

The being wailed as Roark dragged it down the steps to the lab, but it was overwhelmed by the cries of each individual strand alighting on Edar's wrist.

"What are you?" the being shrieked as Roark strapped him to the table.

"What are you?" Byronia asked back.

"Are you one of the slaves from the ship?" Roark asked. "One that the sailors are talking about?"

The being howled and its hair ripped from its roots

and wrapped around its own neck. It squeezed while screaming out its last breaths. The hair turned from gold to gray. The body's flesh desiccated. Edar screamed as the burnt hair on his arm sparked and fells to the stone floor, leaving a raised rash.

"Bring me the salve," Edar panted.

Roark rushed to get the latest salve, applied it gently, and bandaged Edar's arm. Byronia asked, "Is my skin red? Do I have a rash?"

"No. You look a little flush, that's all."

"I believe this is a being from another Realm. Something we haven't seen before. Can you do a dissection? You learn; the Guild learns."

Roark frowned. "This is why Corwin wanted me to see the rash and why you are here."

"Yes. I would've told you, but you didn't ask."

"After our dissection, my lady, we shall go upstairs and have a nice cup of tea, and you can tell us why you brought him to us."

Roark glanced over at his master. "Edar, shouldn't ..."

"Dissection first." Edar gestured at the deteriorating flesh. "We don't seem to have much time. Lady Byronia, would you prefer to take dictation or assist?"

"Assist," she said.

"Very well, Roark, if you would take dictation then? On fresh parchment. I'm sure Lady Byronia will need a copy for your employer," Edar said.

Roark hurried to get a fresh parchment and filled the inkwell. Then he sat at the small desk on the east wall beside the lantern. He sketched out the corpse.

"Cut off the robes but be gentle with the fabric. It too may have secrets."

Byronia undressed the creature. As she removed its inner robes, she said, "I was wrong. This one isn't female, in fact, I see no reproductive organs at all. Perhaps it is like a Telchine?"

"My knowledge of the Telchine is limited," Edar said.

"The Telchine mold their young out of clay and then have a breath of life ritual," Roark said. "They are asexual in nature."

"Have either of you done an autopsy on a Telchine?"

"No," they said together.

"When they die, they turn back into the clay from which they came," Roark said.

"Damn, we could really use an example," Edar said.

"I'm sure someone in the Guild knows the secrets of Telchine life," Roark said.

Edar nodded. "Well, put that in the notes and let's continue. No sexual organs; age: assumed adult. Cause of death self-strangulation with its own hair."

Byronia removed the golden rings it wore on its fingers and in its earlobes. She weighed them and tested the metal. "Gold over nickel" and placed them beside Roark.

Edar weighed and measured the body. "Thirteen stone, Six feet, Nine fingers widths."

"Eyes were lavender, no pupil, growing milky."

"Hair color was gold, but now gray."

Edar looked at the hair through his stacked lenses. "Each hair begins in a small sucker, rather than a follicle." He said. "And ends with a tiny stinger."

"Perhaps that's why the creature started to shed after its death?" Byronia asked. "May we see?" Roark asked.

"Solid hypothesis," Edar stepped away from the stacked lens.

Roark peeked at the hair, sketched it, went back

to his notes. Byronia chewed her inner cheek as her brow rose. Roark wished she wasn't so obvious in displaying her reactions. She was a Guild Diplomat and able to hide her emotions. Why wasn't she?

"The hair is thicker than mine," Edar said. "I'm sorry, dear." He plucked a hair off Byronia's head and examined it. "And yours."

Roark plucked his own hair before his master did it and handed it over.

"That's interesting." Edar said. "Now I don't suppose you'd be willing to part with any body hair?"

Roark slipped his hand under his tunic and found a hair under his arm. He yanked it out. He wished he hadn't groaned at the sting.

"Lowest Realm, lad, we have tweezers."

"Yesterday, you told me this rash might hold life or death. There is no time for tweezers when you're ill," Roark said.

Edar smiled softly as he and Byronia lifted the body and placed a wooden block underneath the torso. "The creature does have enlarged pectorals, but no nipples."

Edar carved into the chest, he curved his scalpel under the pectorals and ran them up to the shoulders, then he peeled back the flesh. Edar sliced into the sides of the corpse, leaving the ribs attached to the breastbone, he removed the entire frontal ribcage as one chest plate.

"Oh, my Gods, Roark, come look," Byronia said.

Roark stood to see inside the body. Long fibrous threads ran under the flesh, intertwining with other threads and ending in a connective web embracing each organ which was covered in small white bumps.

Edar took a needle to the bump. "Papule contains no fluid. Get me jars, milady."

Byronia hurried to the cabinet and came back with labeled jars.

Using a serrated blade, Edar cut through the fibrous threads and placed each organ in a jar of bitter-smelling alcohol. From what Edar called the heart, dripped long viscous strands of blood which coagulated quicker than any blood Roark had ever seen except maybe dwarves.

They slowly moved through each organ within the chest, moving downward to the stomach. "It feels like the creature eats."

"I only observed them drinking wine."

Edar sliced open the stomach, more fibrous material. He put it into the jar. Byronia weighed the filled jar.

Roark's hand cramped from the writing and drawing, but the autopsy continued long into the night.

❄

ROARK SET THE TEA UPON EDAR'S TABLE; Byronia spread another dose of Edar's latest salve over his rash. Roark noticed there was no difference between the red hives now and the first dose.

"I didn't expect I could catch it. It's been so many years since I've had any human disease." Edar asked softly. "Do you think it was your species that protected you tonight?"

"No. I've heard reports of Fairsinge children with the rash. Rentgirls and slaves mostly," Byronia said.

"And my sailor friend said she saw a Fairsinge with the rash and a Daosith on her ship died from it." Roark shuddered. "Do you think it might be the Curse?"

"Perhaps. Or it might just be slower on those with the curse ... who knows?"

"How would we test for that?"

"The only way I can think is something awful,"

Byronia said, her eyes downcast.

"Both of you listen," Edar said, his voice full of every long year in his life and undeath. "We have no time for tea. Byronia, pack the organs and bring them to the Guild House. I'm sure that will help the both of you. But you'll return with information won't you, my girl?"

"Yes, I'll return."

"Good."

"And Roark, you will stay and help me find a cure?"

"Yes."

"Good, then I'll retire. Without rest, no one can heal," Edar said.

Once the cottage was quiet, Roark realized he still hadn't had the chance to look at his Vodnik samples. He found them still wrapped as he left them. He carried them downstairs into the lab for archival purposes. Unfortunately, they had putrefied into thick, foul-smelling water.

✳

Chapter 12
Port Denwort
in the Realm of Dynion

ROARK UNWRAPPED THE BANDAGES FROM Edar's wounded arm. Even overnight, the salve had not tamed the rash. It seemed to be spreading, but Roark hadn't looked closely in the chaos.

"Make another poultice, this time with two parts quicksilver and one-part lanoline and sulfur," Edar said, his voice shrill.

Roark pressed two doses of quicksilver into a jar of lanoline. He tried to hold his breath as he stirred in the sulfur, but the rotten-egg smell assaulted his nose.

Roark spread the new lotion onto the rash. "Feel any better?"

"Perhaps, I can't tell yet."

Edar screamed. Roark saw another welt raise.

"Don't move."

Roark grabbed a skin press – typically used to isolate warts and moles. Quarantining the raised flesh, it was easy to see something wriggling under the skin.

With tweezers, he pulled out a long fibrous hair. They repeated the procedure with each bump, the ones higher on the arm had filaments; the original wound was empty.

"Perhaps it was the quicksilver ... maybe it ran from the quicksilver," Roark said. "Our traditional cures might be spreading it ... "

Edar's ashen face grew even more pallid. "I don't know what will become of me, but take my works and go."

"But the transmutation ... "

"I don't know those secrets."

"But I brought something, many things from my journeys ... " Under Roark's tunic, the quartz trembled. *Be still!*

Roark ignored it. "I just didn't get the chance to show you. Lord Corwin gave me Lady Daena's journal!" He removed the quartz from under his shirt and handed it to him then ran into his room for the book. "Daena's dead, but before she died, Corwin believes she moved her soul into another body."

Edar didn't move from his chair. His eyes were focused on the quartz of his former colleague and friend. "Why didn't you tell me immediately?"

"You cut me off ... you wanted to find a cure ... "

Edar gripped the quartz until his knuckles grew white. "Get out of my sight."

Roark did not fear Edar, but the look of utter betrayal upon the lich's face crushed him. He reached for the book and Edar swatted his hand away. "Leave it."

He went to Edar's mother's room, changed into traveling gear and packed. He wondered what Corwin would think of his failure.

"Where do you think you're going?" Edar asked when Roark stepped from the room.

"Home, until the Guild calls again."

"Never mind that. Go to David and see if he knows of anyone willing to give me their body. Otherwise, you'll be buying a slave. Hurry now. Who knows how much time I have left?"

Not bothering to change, Roark dashed to Mayor Kleidmacher's main gate. The footman smiled and greeted Roark warmly.

"I must see the Mayor, good sir." Roark bowed his head. "Edar Candlewick is close to death."

The footman looked surprised but announced Roark.

Mayor Kleidmacher greeted him with a small incline of his head from his chair, his silver cane sitting beside him. In a weak, wheezy voice, the mayor said, "Now what's this about Edar?"

Roark perched on a velvet cushioned bench. "Edar contacted a rash from a patient. He was shocked, as he believed he was immune from most human diseases. My master believes we have learned the recipe for transmutation, but the spell is violent."

"And you need?"

"A healthy body. The spell calls for someone no longer clinging to life—perhaps wracked by guilt. Edar will try it on himself once we have the man."

Hoping that it would be a criminal, Roark added, "But as a Guild member, Mister Mayor, I believe we choose someone who won't be missed. It wouldn't be good if I heard this through the Guild grapevine."

Kleidmacher tapped his wrinkled finger to a grizzled chin. "I might know someone. A firstborn of eighteen. Family's had trouble with him since he was a lad. But if it works, Lord Roark?"

Self-reproach dripped into Roark's soul. "You can be the next served, Mister Mayor. Edar has long been grateful for your patronage."

"Good. Strange folks are coming to Port Denwort; the city needs a stronger mayor to ensure our protection. I'll get Edar the body. Tell him to be at home, first thing in the morning."

❊

Chapter 13
Port Denwort
in the Realm of Dynion

"MY SON ... ANYTHING YOU CAN DO," THE farmwife said between sobs.

"I cannot guarantee my remedies will help Thomas." Edar acted like a stern apothecary to the farmers, but Roark saw the wanton gleam that he tried to hide. "And it is a dangerous procedure."

Remorse stained Roark's heart. Corwin had been right. Edar was still the man who bought Kian to do medical tests. When given the chance, he experimented upon his own people. Roark wanted to tell the family to run far away from this house and never come back, but the words caught in his throat. If Edar didn't have a new body, he might die. Why aren't the answers as easy as they once were?

Roark wondered if these questions would ever end.

"You may find him quite changed by the procedure," Edar said. "How do you feel about that?"

The farmwife's callused hands rubbed together in worry. She leaned her wiry shoulder upon on her sturdy husband for support. His calm brown eyes scanned the parlor. He was rather short for a human, but even at fifty, the man had good posture and a strong jawline. The son took after his father though his shoulders were hunched, and his eyes never left the floor.

"A change would be good," the farmhusband said.

The son whispered, "I want to go home."

"And do what?" his father said. "Continue to cause your mother's pain?"

The farmwife's crumpled to her knees. Tears spilled freely down her cheeks as she sobbed louder. Roark wondered if his mother would ever cry for him like that. Probably not.

Edar jumped into chivalrous action. He kneeled before her as the human knights kneel before their queen. "Sweet farmer, do not weep. I swear I will do all in my power to bring your son's body back to health. But I must warn you of the danger. Let me call for a cup of chamomile to soothe your nerves."

"Master Candlewick, that won't be necessary." The farmhusband helped his wife to her feet.

"I believe it is," Edar said. "Lord Roark, be a dear; would you see to the poor woman's comfort."

Roark inclined his head. The farmerwife's eyes opened wide. "A lord?"

"Yes, I earned my lordship from my family and am here to learn remedies. Now if you please, good farmwife. My master grows his own herbs. A bit of chamomile will ease your suffering."

Roark listened as Edar and the farmhusband spoke in hushed voices, but he couldn't make out every word. Once the farmwife and her son were seated in the kitchen and had piping cups of chamomile, Roark hurried back to the men.

The farmhusband glanced at the kitchen door. "The boy's too dreamy and listless for good sense. His carelessness while bailing hay caused injury to another of our children. He doesn't eat nor sleep, due to guilt, rather than illness. I think he's needing a job away from the farm, more than your remedies."

"Is your other child alive?" Roark asked.

"A visible scar and a limp, but what's that? She's a

thrifty, common-sense girl. She'll make a great farmer."

Roark opened his mind to the family. The father's emotions and words did not match on the matter. The scar and limp were a reminder to them all. This man loved his son, but he had not forgiven him for the accident. Though she wanted to protect her son from pain, she had not forgiven him either. And Thomas hated himself.

Edar's eyes danced. "Perhaps, my good farmer, I could give the boy a job in my garden? My apprentice and I are often too busy to keep things in good repair. I've plenty of room to keep him. What arrangements would ease your goodwife's heart?"

❊

ROARK GASPED AS HE OPENED THE WINDOW. Thomas raked the garden without his tunic covering his chest. His chiseled muscles were refined from his life on the farm. As with most healthy human males, his shoulders were broader than Roark's, and they would grow to be broader still. At least in terms of aesthetics, he approved of Edar's choice. But there must be a better way.

Edar knocked on the door. "I heard from Lady Byronia. She returns tonight, and I brought you fresh linens, my friend; the laundress comes today." He set a basket of herbs on the floor, then moved to strip the bed, but Roark hurried to do it.

"Thank you. I'm forgiven then?" Roark asked gathering the old sheets.

"Yes." Edar replaced the old wolfsbane and lavender with new herbs.

"How is the rash?"

"No change." Gazing upon Thomas in the garden, Edar whispered, "Were you enjoying the view?"

Roark felt heat rise to face. "Yes."

"Good. And do you think the beautiful Lady B. might enjoy Thomas's form?"

The warmth was sucked from Roark's chest. The idea an old man might be interested in Byronia disgusted him. Still, careful his tone remained smooth, he said, "She has a consort."

"Who is he?"

"I've ever seen him once. All I know is Corwin ensured she wouldn't bear his children. Corwin called him a common layabout."

"What does he look like?"

"He has the pale skin common to my people and dark hair, but I wouldn't know the man if I saw him."

"Well then, Thomas has dark hair, and once he is away from the sun, his skin will pale," Edar said. "Unless you believe she doesn't enjoy humans."

Hearing the hollow ring in Edar's tone, Roark said, "I've no idea. I could ask my sister, she'd know."

"It doesn't matter. There are many beautiful women in the Seven Realms."

"Are you sure this is how you want to do it? I could do more research. We could find a different way."

"The spell says the body must be unloved, does it not?"

"Yes." Roark knew he had lost by the sour taste in his mouth.

"We have everything we need. I have waited for this moment for over fifty years."

"But I fear for you."

"I know, my friend. I fear too, but I believe it will work. Lady Byronia will arrive this evening, and we can begin. Once you are finished in here, prepare the lab."

*

Chapter 14
Port Denwort
in the Realm of Dynion

ROARK STOOD AT THE TOP OF THE CELLAR stairs. He did not want to go through the violent madness of the transmutation ritual. Yet, this is what Edar wanted and what Corwin ordered him to do. Roark took a step at a time until he reached the stone floor of the cellar. Even with the four lanterns pointed on the central table, it was still too shadowy.

As Edar instructed, Byronia put sage and rosemary in four small copper pots and lit them until they smoked. The smoke from sage and rosemary filled the laboratory. Edar placed a mirrored amulet around Roark's neck; Byronia wore a matching one.

Edar let his robe drop to the floor. He stood naked in front of Thomas Farmer who lay strapped to the central gurney.

"Let me go. I won't tell anyone. Let me go," Thomas whimpered.

Compassion burned in Roark for the young man. In his head, he repeated, Thomas injured his sister. He brought this on himself.

Edar carefully connected the motor's copper rods to the metal table and to the water wheel on the other side.

Shuffling across the stone floor, Roark lay a line of salt around the gurneys and cast a circle of protection.

"Well then, Roark, Byronia, tonight we dance!"

Edar raised his hands and with a loud, clear voice called, "The Seraphim of the Resurrection will no longer look upon me. I take Thomas Farmer's body as my own. I will purify and perfect this body by giving it a good man's soul. He has been forsaken by his parents and put into my upkeep. His body is my own, and I claim it."

Thomas screamed, "No! Let me go!" The smell of urine filled the cellar.

On Edar's signal, Byronia poured a bucket of icy salt water over Thomas's body. Kicking against the leather straps and shifting his torso on the metal table, the young man struggled against his bonds. On Edar's signal, she moved to the stairs in case it all went wrong.

Roark turned the crank which rotated the motor. A high-pitched tone engulfed the room, which settled into a low hum. The rise of electricity tickled Roark's corpuscles. Sparks danced across the copper rods to the metal table. Thomas whimpered as electrical shocks and tiny lightning bursts frolicked over him. Roark turned the crank faster; the hum grew louder. Thomas fell back; his heart stopped beating.

"His body looks good." Edar touched the carotid artery and checked for a pulse. He did not hide the delight and excitement in his voice. He poured icy water over his own head and lay naked shoulder to shoulder with the dead lad. Electricity danced over both of them. Edar's body trembled and reacted to each shock, but his maniacal laughter echoed off the stone walls.

"Let me hear through Thomas Farmer's ears." Edar cried out as he sliced off his left ear which flopped onto the floor in a bloody mess. His whole body convulsed, he vomited into a bucket onto the floor.

Roark wanted to puke in reaction to Edar's vomit,

but he did not. He was an assassin. Instead, he hurried to bring him a flagon of fresh water.

"No, finish it! I will embrace the pain! Let me walk with Thomas Farmer's feet." Edar stabbed himself in the feet and screamed again, He dropped the knife which clattered against the wet stone floor "Finish it, Roark, finish it!"

Roark picked up the knife.

"Edar ... "

"Let me taste through Thomas Farmer's tongue." Edar sliced through the flesh of the tongue, and a bubble of blood and spit came from Edar's open mouth. "I can't go on, finish ... Let me see through Thomas Farmer's eyes! Roark, do it! Help me!"

Roark didn't move.

Through blood and spittle, Edar shouted, "Don't leave me in torment, let me see through Thomas Farmer's eyes!"

Roark clenched his dagger and took Edar's eyes. The empty stare out of the bloody orbs was the worst thing the young lord ever saw. His knees weakened.

"I embrace the pain!" Edar screamed.

Roark lost track of time as the bloody ritual went on. Edar whispered what he would do with the farm boy's stomach, hands, arms, legs. Roark stabbed him in those places. The ritual ended with the phrase, "Let me love with Thomas Farmer's heart." Roark stabbed the appropriate place on Edar's chest. The knife entered cleanly.

As Roark withdrew the blade, blood spurted out and flowed over each corpse. Roark opened Thomas's mouth, so Edar's spirit had an easy entry.

Roark turned the crank and electricity danced over the blood and water.

Nothing happened.

"Edar!" Roark rotated the crank harder, more

electricity danced over the two bodies. "Come back, brother, come back!" The motor's humming pinched Roark's brain. Edar was an old man, and his body had been weak with undeath.

Edar's spirit rose from his body but discovered it was covered in blood.

"Spirit of Edar Candlewick, live again in the body of Thomas Farmer!" Roark ordered.

"I am an old soul and must be cleaned for resurrection," the spirit said.

"Edar Candlewick, remember we bring forth this vessel for you."

Roark poured a pitcher over water over the young man.

"Unclean!" It howled, but the spirit of Edar slid into the young man's open mouth.

Roark's shoulders ached, he turned the crank faster until sparks leapt off the bodies and danced across the bloody floor.

On the table, the body started to moan. The moaning became screaming. But it wasn't just the farm boy and the necromancer. It seemed as all their past lives wept in a bleating egophony of sorrow and rebirth.

Roark smashed his hands to his ears trying to quiet the unending sound. He fell to the floor and clenched his eyes shut. Byronia came and wrapped her arms around his head and pulled him close to her.

The arcane book said nothing of this sound! He wanted to run, but he owed it to Edar to stay. Not knowing what else to do, Roark began counting. There were sixty seconds in a minute. Three hundred seconds in five minutes. In five minutes, he would take Byronia by the hand and run upstairs. They would wash off the blood, pack and get the lowest Realm out of Edar's cottage.

"Roark, Byronia!" Edar groaned in Thomas's voice. "Are you there?"

Roark opened his eyes and saw Edar straining Thomas's head toward the ceiling.

"Release me."

Roark stood and approached the gurneys. "It worked! Dear Gods and Goddess, you are here!" Hands trembling, Roark hurried to unlatch the leather straps. Edar rose from the table in Thomas's perfect young body. "It worked. I feel more alive than ever before!" Edar said, moving up the stairs. "Feed me, I'm starving, then let us dance!"

The idea of eating or dancing repulsed Roark. He caught Byronia's eye. "I think we need a bath first," she said. "And it is nearly dawn, perhaps it would be better if we went tomorrow?"

Edar looked down at his naked, bloodstained flesh and laughed. "Right as usual, my friends."

❊

Chapter 15
Port Denwort
in the Realm of Dynion

"I CAN'T BELIEVE THE CHANGE IN YOU, Edar," Mayor Kleidmacher said, the envy apparent in his wheezing voice, his tanned face no longer grandfatherly as he tapped Edar's leg with his cane.

"Find me another body, David, and you will be next," Edar said and leaned over to his oldest friend and squeezed his hand.

The mayor smiled. "Oh, I've already chosen the body."

Roark noticed a change in the tapestry, a different number of figures were in the Waters of Resurrection. He knew he could protect himself from the mayor; he believed he and Byronia could fight their way out if need be.

However, there was no violence forthcoming. The footman entered the room and said, "Lunch is served, Mister Mayor."

"Excellent, excellent." He rose and tapped the wall with his cane. Leaning close, to Edar, he wheezed, "My grandson might be a good mayor someday. He's still a youth of one and twenty."

"The demons that you know." Edar winked.

Lowest Realm, Roark thought. He smiled and nodded and pretended that he was on board. Byronia also seemed to be on board, but then, Byronia could be hiding her true feelings on the matter. *Dear Goddess, I hope Byronia is on the same side as me.*

※

WITH A LIGHT SQUEEZE ON BYRONIA'S silk covered forearm, Edar said, "It's a magical night. I could dance forever."

Roark agreed. It was a lovely evening. The falling sun reflected off the water, casting the whole world in pink and the palest blue. In the distance, they could hear the songs of gulls as they nested for the evening.

The three-story brick and beam Black Lion looked well-kept from the outside, and laughter could be heard from within as they approached. Edar stepped in front of them to hold the heavy-looking wooden door for Byronia and Roark as they entered the tavern.

A minstrel in a scarlet doublet played a light melody as human men and women danced in the middle of the room. At the bar, several men drank ale and, in the corner, an elderly woman clapped her hands to the song. Edar's face never stopped grinning as he led them to a table next to the fire. Roark frowned.

Roark wondered if he ought to mention Edar's earlier desires to Byronia, but what could he say? And what business was his? Edar had grown young, and, in years, Byronia's body was older than Edar's.

"What's wrong, my friend?" Edar asked.

"Nothing, strange thoughts is all."

A jovial maid scuttled over. She side-eyed Roark with approval as she curtsied. "Welcome, milady, milords. The elfkin are always welcome at the Black Lion."

"Thank you," Byronia said.

"Will you be dining with us tonight?"

"Yes. Do you still have the roasted pig with stewed apples?" Edar asked.

The maid brought their dinner, massive ham steaks smothered in stewed apples and cherries. Edar ate with the delight of a freed soul. Bottles of wine were brought to their table, which Edar guzzled cup after cup until his eyes swam and every word reeked of sour booze.

"This is a silly request, but will you dance with me, my lady?" Edar asked. He placed his palm upwards.

"Yes." Byronia placed her hand upon his. They joined the dancers on the floor. Edar circled forward while Byronia circled the opposite direction.

After three paces the dancers stopped and bowed to each other. They laughed as they spun. Roark felt the wideness of the Expanse at that moment. He missed the fellowship he once had with Eohan and Kian.

He must choose between life and his Great Work. He would learn from Edar but also learn from his mistakes. He certainly wouldn't put the people he loved in such pain. He would never choose to transmute the way Edar did, but there had to be another way. A better way.

Roark's thoughts were interrupted by Byronia grabbing his hands. "Come." She pulled him into the dancers.

Roark scanned the crowds until he found Edar speaking to a rosy-complexioned girl in a white dress.

"Focus." Byronia hissed into his ear. "Look who just entered. They took the table next to the bar."

Roark saw them: the new species. Their hair moving about the human and dwarf rentgirls as if it had a mind of its own.

"Let's go to another pub, my friends," Edar said, his hands about the girl in the white dress.

"Edar, look. There in the corner."

He glanced over his shoulder. "This is a night of

magic, not of sorrow." And he and the girl in the white dress drunkenly stumbled outside.

Byronia went to the bar and paid. "Um, Roark, I'm sorry to ask, but you might need to get the next tab."

"What do you mean?"

"Edar's drunk, and in his state, he'll be no good to us anyway. Ensure he gets home safely. I'll keep watch here."

❋

Chapter 16
Port Denwort
in the Realm of Dynion

EDAR STARED AT THE HALF-NAKED GIRL asleep, twisted amongst the sheets, her white dress and ripped stockings on the floor. He noted a handprint on her shoulder. He hoped he hadn't done it but had no idea. He didn't even know her name.

He crawled out of bed and looked at his new face in the mirror. How lovely and full of life he was. How flush his cheeks were. How his eyes sparkled. His chest though still slender would fill out in the next few years.

It had been many decades since his organ functioned, but he assumed most of the rules of courtship remained the same. He hurried to the kitchen to make her breakfast; that's what a good paramour did. He must make his beloved feel loved—maybe he could ask Roark to reintroduce himself and learn her name.

He wished it didn't feel like a million spiders crept up his new flesh. Pulsing with the lifeblood flowing through his veins and oxygen through his lungs, Edar paced his kitchen. He sat on his wooden chair without the creak of old joints, but pleasure was overtaken by the strange sensation that someone else was behind his eyes. He quickly scrawled in his tome:

This young body is but a mask for an old soul, and I am not alone in the shell. Thomas is still here. I need to find a spell to disperse his soul to the Waters of Resurrection.

His stomach growled. "The Work isn't done," His body trembled violently. He stumbled down the hall. He collapsed. The first tears fell from Edar's eyes in nearly thirty years.

"Roark," he called.

Minutes later, the young man appeared. Edar realized their bodies were the same age.

"I'm ill. Make me a sleeping draft."

"Is this what happened last time? When you became a lich?"

"I don't remember, but I don't remember the neighbor's conversations being so loud. I feel everything, my heartbeat, the blood in my veins. I remember everything. My life as Edar, my life as a revenant. I feel I have new eyes, new ears. I want to experience more. Yet, I'm terrified. And I don't remember her name!"

Roark's footsteps crossed the stone floor. Edar covered his ears. Why was the boy being so loud? He could walk in silence, why wasn't he? Roark lifted him to his feet.

"Whose name?"

"The girl in my room."

"Sara. She's a rent girl."

"Not a paramour?"

"I'm sorry. I suppose she could be if you loved her."

"You're such a romantic. I wanted to make her some current bread, but if she's a rentgirl ... " The wetness ran down his cheek. "Where is Byronia?"

"We saw some of them. She stayed to gather more intel."

"Oh." A strange sensation filled Edar's aching heart. No one loves me. Maybe no one ever had. Was Roark even his friend or was he here for his own Great

Work? I want to see Mama. But the image that rose in his mind was not of the former apothecary, but of the farmer.

Roark embraced him about the shoulders. "Are you alright? I'll stay beside you and help you with whatever you need."

"Until the Guild calls," Edar said bitterly.

"Well, I need to work, but not today," Roark said. "And we'll do whatever you want."

"Well, first, I need to figure out how to wake that girl and get her out of here. What if mama sees her!"

"Edar, your mother is dead."

"What, yes, yes." Edar shook his head. He was a grown man. He had lived over a century. What was wrong with him? He cleared his throat. "Roark, you must ensure I don't wander off to my parents' house. I mean Thomas's parents' house. He misses his mother. I guess we have those things in common. Or perhaps it is my memory of my own mother that woke him. He's still here."

"Perhaps we should work on a new salve?"

"New salve?"

"For the rash? Remember Port Welliver burned. You know how to create salves and remedies, Thomas doesn't. Be more you."

Edar no longer cared about the salve or the sickness, but he nodded. It was something to do. "Yes, good idea." Crossing the room to his safe, he asked, "Roark, do you know how much I owe her? Or the going rate for such activities?"

Roark shook his head. "In Fairdhel, such things are discussed in advance. Um, try a half-sovereign, and if it's not enough maybe a full one. Increase by a tenth."

Edar slipped back into his room. The girl still slept. He shook her shoulder. She rubbed the sleep from her eyes. "Can I offer you breakfast? My associate and I

95

need to get to work."

He held out a half-sovereign and knew he'd already overpaid by the excitement that spread over her face. She took it and quickly dressed. He watched her, mostly looking for the rash which he didn't see. *Thank the Gods, I just got this new body. I'll need to be more careful.*

"I hope you enjoyed it?" he asked her.

"I always enjoy a tumble," she said.

A sour feeling lined Edar's throat, he stopped her at the door. He gave her another half.

"Did you want something else?" she asked sweetly.

"No, but listen, a new disease is coming to Port Denwort. Be safe out there. Or stop doing what you're doing if you can."

"Ha, so you're one of those." She snatched the half-crown out of his hand and slammed the door as she left.

❊

Chapter 17
Port Denwort
in the Realm of Dynion

EDAR AND ROARK CONCOCTED SEVEN NEW salves. The day had been uneventful until Edar excused himself. Minutes later, Roark heard a crash from Edar's room. He hurried inside to find Edar on the floor, punching his mirror which dented the polished brass until it was unusable.

"What are you doing?"

Edar looked at him with rage in his eyes. He grabbed his stool and hurtled it towards Roark who backed into the hallway before it crashed into the door jam and broke into pieces.

"He's taking me over!" Edar grabbed a grooming blade off his dressing table. He cut his bare chest. "He wants me out."

Roark grabbed Edar's wrist and disarmed him. The knife clattered against the wooden floor.

Roark grabbed an undertunic off the floor and pressed it to the wound, ignoring the perspiration and stench of chemicals.

"Help me."

"Let's get you back in the kitchen. It'll be alright. We'll find the answer."

"You may have to kill me," Edar whispered. "Thomas gently knocks on each brain cell as he gains control of my body."

"No, I won't. We'll get through this." Roark lifted Edar from below his arm and half-dragged him back to the kitchen.

"You're a guild assassin. Killing is what you do. If I lose control, I might hurt someone: Byronia for example or maybe even Alana."

"No, you won't. I know you won't. I've seen her future."

"Will you look into my future?"

"Yes, but not until you are better, my friend. It takes much out of me and right now you need me at my best."

Edar nodded. "It's been so many years since I had someone to rely upon. Thank you for staying."

A rush of protectiveness filled Roark's heart, and he suddenly wondered why he was so adamant before about not wanting a child. Maybe he did want one. Not now, but who was to say what would happen in five years. Edar and his experiments would go on. Maybe by then, Roark would have a consort.

In Edar's current form, he might take a wife. They would have someone to take care of and to take care of them and any children.

The quartz dug into his flesh: *Do not look into the future; stay here and tell Edar that this is what you saw. Give him hope.*

❋

Chapter 18
Port Denwort
in the Realm of Dynion

TRYING TO FIND A SOLUTION, ROARK PACED in Edar's mother's room. Every piece of furniture had turned foreign and cruel. Roark penned a letter to Alana to ask for help, but couldn't send it. *Alana would hate me if she knew what we did to Thomas. I betrayed my friendship with Kian and Eohan by taking the boy's body and giving it to Edar. How could I do this? How could I? There has to be another way. This is not the Work. This is the opposite. This is slavery of the worst kind.*

He walked to Mayor Kleidmacher's house.

"Edar's symptoms have taken a turn for the worse," he said to the footman.

The footman hurried inside to deliver the message.

"The mayor has more pressing matters," The footman said, "but agrees to see you for a few minutes."

The mayor met Roark in the hallway instead of the parlor. He noted the grandson with a pretty girl a few years younger beside him on the divan inside. By her hair, she was still a maiden, perhaps the grandson's betrothed. Thinking of the mayor's old hands upon that sweet-looking girl, he inwardly vowed, *I will not be part of this.*

The quartz shocked him. *What does it matter who the human mayor is? These aren't even your people.*

99

Roark wondered why he cared about some young couple he didn't even know, but Edar's symptom's remained in the forefront of his mind. He quickly informed the mayor of their lack of progress.

Mayor Kleidmacher cocked his head to the side and glanced over his shoulder. "Keep me informed, Lord Roark. I do not take broken favors lightly."

Once out of the house, Roark went to the mayor's stables, saddled his dear mare and led Jaci from the stables down the dirty streets of Port Denwort to the Golden Sea. She was not happy about the downgraded residence, but it wasn't the worse place she'd slept, and the stablehands were Guild trained.

Roark kicked a pebble as he shuffled into the public house. *Who do I work for? Corwin, Mayor Kleidmacher, Edar? I work for myself. This is my journey.*

Under his shirt, the quartz vibrated. He pulled it from his tunic and gazed within its depths. More ancient than he even in its current form, the pendant knew what he had done, but didn't care.

"You lived before the Schism."

And I'll live long after. The old man told you to learn. Why do you think that is?

The quartz's knowledge flooded his mind.

"Because the Eighth Realm beings are coming," Roark said. "Edar's transmutation is only to learn what they do."

Byronia came beside him. "Roark, what are you doing?"

Roark quickly slipped the chain under his tunic. "Considering all that happened last night."

She put up her fingers, and the barkeep poured two pints of mead. The barkeep led them to a private room before he realized they weren't in the main room anymore.

She sat down on the long bench and gestured for

him to sit beside her as the barkeep set down their mead and left.

"What's going on? Are you lost in a vision?"

"No, I mean I don't know, but Edar's dying."

Byronia pursed her lips and held his hand tightly. "It isn't your fault you were doing as he asked."

"But Thomas didn't ask for this, and he is angry."

"No, he didn't." Byronia sighed. "Nor did I, nor did you. I'm taking the hair to the Guild House. Come with me. Leave this madness."

Roark shook his head. "I can't leave Edar. Will you tell your uncle all that we learned over the past nights? I'd rather not see him right now."

"If it pleases you." She reached out and touched his hand. "We'll live long beyond this day. I believe we both have foreseen that."

Roark blinked and met her sapphire eyes. "Did Corwin ever hit you?"

She shrugged. "A few slaps across the head when I was an apprentice. Mostly as long as I respected his position he didn't care what I did or how quickly I learned. And he grabbed me once as an adult and threatened me. That frightened me, but he didn't hurt me."

He rubbed the quartz under his shirt. This time it did not or could not offer advice. "What I'm trying to ask is: you don't fear him beating our daughter or anything like that?"

"You saw her?"

Roark nodded.

"Of course not. Corwin will love her, but his mistakes will be on her shoulders. If she dies, he will kill himself, which will begin the chain reaction through the Guild Houses and Seven Realms will crumble."

"He kills her?"

Byronia's eyes grew distant. "He is only responsible through inadvertence, but he is a House Master first and foremost. If I leave her to his care, she will stand alone, and the curse's madness will creep into her. But her father won't let her stand alone. If she does not fall, she is or will be the War Ender to save us. I have already gone beyond the Seven Realms; your work is important or will be. Why is speaking about visions so maddening? I looked at all the paths. So many paths ... "

"I'm not sure I want to be a father."

"Then why did you ask me for a child?"

"I ask you?"

"Yes." She shook her head and her eyes settled upon him. "At least you did in the vision, but maybe by having this conversation we changed the future, and I ask you. Now would you like me to move Jaci? I already moved Joy. If you fear for her safety, the Golden Sea won't protect her if it comes from the mayor. Guild trained staff, indeed."

✳

Chapter 19
Port Denwort
in the Realm of Dynion

THOMAS AWOKE UNDER STRANGE SHEETS IN a strange room, everything was too neat and well-kept for him to be at the farm. The young man shivered as if a spider skittered up his back. He rubbed his hands on his arms as acid roiled in his stomach. He burped. Dryness coated his mouth, and sour wine lingered on his tongue. Homesick for the taste of his mother's chicken soup, Thomas slipped out of bed and went to the window.

In the reflection, he could almost detect the monster trapped in his body. The old lich clung to him and slowly eroded his soul, but he couldn't see where it was or the damage it was causing. He must escape before madness descended again.

Ma had wept at our parting. He thought of his father who used to lift him on his shoulders and exclaim that his entire allotment would one day be Thomas's. He missed his younger sister's songs and his brother's games. The three worked the farm with their parents, played together and bickered until the accident. He knew he couldn't go back, but he had to let his sister know he forgave her for taking all that was once his. And hoped she forgave him for taking what was hers. If he could only find peace before the monster came back.

He sat in the soft bed. Beside him, still sleeping was not his little brother, but an elfkin with red hair. They were about the same age, but Thomas feared him as an enemy. He didn't know how or why, he just feared him.

He crept out of bed and crossed the room to the window. It was still night. Thomas's hands trembled as he undid the latch. He swung open the window wide and jumped down into the herb garden trampling a lavender bush.

Glancing around, he decided he must be in a townhome's garden. No one in the country did so little with land. The only animals were mice and nightbirds. He crept past the rosebushes to the garden fence when the elfkin tackled him from behind.

Thomas spat out dirt from his mouth and cried, "Let me go!"

"Edar, wake up!"

Thomas jerked upwards and tried to rise, but was surprised by the elfkin's strength. The elfkin pulled him to his feet and gripped Thomas's arm behind his back and squeezed. He shoved two fingers into Thomas's armpit, forcing the other boy to move or crumple with agony. "Why do you do this?"

"Edar, you are unwell."

"My name's Thomas! Let me go."

The elfkin shoved him through the garden door and into the kitchen where Thomas was sprawled onto the kitchen floor. "Thomas, then, you are unwell. I am Roark. I am your friend."

"Get away from me." Scrambling across the room, Thomas grabbed a cup off the shelf and threw it at him. Roark dodged it, caught him again and opened the cellar door.

Thomas cried out in terror as his feet hit the stairs. "No, don't take me down there."

Blackness was below him. He elbowed backward, he pulled and pushed, but the elfkin was too strong. Roark slapped him across the face.

"Edar. Wake up. Damn you, Edar." Each step, they were lower into the earth. The cellar door was more distant, escape more unlikely. Thomas's feet hit the stone ground.

Ignoring the agony, Thomas ripped his arms away. The intense pain radiated from his shoulders to his entire torso and down his legs. He made it to the steps. Roark had hold of him again, twisted him around and knocked him onto a metal table.

Thomas screamed as leather straps went over his wrists. He kicked upwards hard but connected with nothing. Roark had one leg down, and then the next. Another strap went over his chest.

The light came on. Unspeakable atrocities lined the wall in jars and beside him, Roark crumpled to his knees and muttered, "What have I done?"

"I'll kill you."

Roark didn't answer.

"Let me go; let me see my mother."

Roark looked up then with a pained stare. "Your mother?"

Thomas nodded. He had a single moment of hope that the elfkin might release him until he felt the monster behind his eyes, growing stronger. Devouring him, his memories until all he could see was his mother crying. "My mother misses me. No. No. No."

Edar broke through Thomas's frightened and bitter mind and retook the body. He wasn't surprised to find himself strapped to his own gurney, Roark's blue eyes looking down on him in concern. "Are you alright?"

"It seems Thomas wasn't contrite enough, or two grown souls can't be in the same body. Find me another."

"But ... "

"Go now, I don't know how long I can keep control."

Roark unlatched him and scurried up the stairs. His footfalls pounding against the wood. He slammed the door to the cellar behind him, Edar winced at the thundering sounds. He slipped off the gurney and went to make himself a bath.

❄

IT WAS NOT YET DAWN AS ROARK WANDERED through the shop-lined streets. Above the shops were the homes of merchants. The wealthiest had multiple floors reaching to the sky, the poorest only an apartment over their shop. He could slip in and steal one even before they knew he did it, but these people were protected by Mayor Kleidmacher. If he was caught killing out of contract, the Guild would be informed. He would be crucified.

He had seen the fear in Thomas's eyes. He had seen the love he had for his family. That is why the spell ultimately failed.

Huddled between allies and under the docks in numbers for safety and warmth, urchins still slept. Some looked healthy enough for Edar. Some might be healthy enough in a month with good food and warm clothing. No one would miss an orphaned, homeless child, even one of their own number, but Roark couldn't attack a defenseless child. *I became an assassin so I would not be responsible for the loss of innocents.* He turned away.

As the sun rose, all around him people woke to morning chores. Slaves were running errands for their masters and mistresses as the shopkeepers opened their shops. These people were innocent, just like the laundress had been when the Vodnik Lord found her. He had become the Vodnik lord.

The quartz pendant quivered against his flesh and pulsed energy into him. *Stop overreacting.*

"Stop overreacting," he muttered to himself.

In the alleys, several rentboys and girls were chattering about the night's take. Roark found a rentboy who hadn't left the corner yet who looked to be about eighteen with tanned skin. His hair was brown but looked golden in the morning light as did his eyes. He was a few fingers taller than Roark, perhaps he might grow a few fingers more with proper nutrition. His limbs were slender, but he might have some muscles if he worked at it. And since his clothing was sparse, Roark could see no sign of the rash. He would do.

"Do you service men?" Roark asked.

"I service anyone willing to pay," the rentboy said in the casual tired tone of one who hadn't slept all night.

"Ever go to a private residence? My master ... would ... pay ... "

The words caught in Roark's throat. He turned around and walked away. He couldn't do it. The quartz shocked his bare flesh, but Roark couldn't steal another innocent life. He failed.

※

Chapter 20
Port Denwort
in the Realm of Dynion

"NO ONE WOULD DO?" EDAR ASKED, HIS voice strained as he mixed a pottage on the stove. The rich fragrance of garlic, lavender, basil over vegetables filled the room and made Roark's empty stomach growl.

"I'm sorry, I didn't find someone ridden with guilt or anyone who hated life. I thought about bringing you an urchin, but that would bring its own problems. Who would come to a child for remedies?" Roark leaned his elbow on the table to prop up his head. A short nap would get him through the day, but first, he needed food.

"I guess you're right. Still, once you get some rest, would you go out looking again? Perhaps you can bring a Guild mark to me? No one would miss them—and I'm sure you have some skill in making one wish for death."

Roark's stomach dropped. "I suppose so." He hoped the evasion wasn't apparent.

Edar scraped the sides of the pot with his wooden spoon. "Could I have a donation to sustain me? If I'm strong, I can keep control better."

"Yes, of course. After breakfast?"

"I hoped I could get it now. Thomas is behind my eyes. I fear I will fall into madness or he will drag me down with him." Edar rested his hand upon Roark's who felt the tremble. *A young hand shouldn't tremble so much. Edar must be suffering.*

With his last burst of energy, Roark gathered the components of the potion. He sliced open his wrist and watched blood drip into the ceramic cup until he closed his eyes.

Edar nudged him.

He looked down at the cup; it was full.

Edar finished the potion and drank deeply. Roark couldn't see any change upon his youthful countenance, but he stood straighter and whistled as he moved back to the stove. *That must be a good sign.*

Edar set a bowl down in front of Roark. "I know we'll find someone. I know it. Tuck in now."

Roark leaned over the steaming bowl and inhaled the savory aroma before he took a large spoonful. The sausage was spiced perfectly; the potatoes had taken in some of the flavor of the herbs. His second bite was bigger than the first.

Roark felt his eyelids droop. He glanced across the table at Edar who smiled at him. He realized Edar hadn't touched his own bowl.

A stupor washed over him. His head hit the table, and his body hit the wooden floor. Blackness took him.

✳

THOMAS HOOKED ROARK'S ARM OVER HIS shoulder and dragged the unconscious body to the cellar door. Edar hadn't wanted it to be like this, but Thomas had to escape. As the two souls fought for supremacy, it felt like millions of spiders crawling on his brain. And it was his brain.

The monster needed a home and Thomas already understood the monster's weakness for beautiful things. The whore, his elfkin companions, even the elaborately carved brass mirror which Thomas had destroyed. If Roark wished to give the monster a body, then the monster could have Roark's. He forced a thought to their shared mind. *As Lord Roark, you might have the beautiful Lady Byronia.* It was a risk.

"Check for weapons," Thomas said.

Edar followed Thomas's will. Thomas felt the invader's sadness that Roark trusted him so much he remained unarmed in his home.

Thomas reminded Edar of his loneliness.

"Who knows an elfkin body might work better than a human's anyway?" Edar said.

Carefully taking the stairs step by step, Edar moved backward into the darkness, dragging Roark under the arms.

✳

ROARK WOKE FEELING EVERY BUMP OF THE stairs as Edar dragged Roark into the darkness. He didn't know if it had been moments or hours. Another bump, another step. He opened his eyes. Sweat poured off Edar's brow and soaked his silk robe. Roark tried to plan an attack, but his mind was murky from Edar's drugs. The body might have been made strong by farm work, but he wasn't a fighter.

No plan, just attack.

At the bottom of the steps, Edar let him go. He went to the table. Roark rose to his feet, his balance still off, but his muscles remembered his training. *I must attack, I must not give quarter.* Roark grabbed the mirror amulet which had been left on the north wall cupboard and slipped it around his neck. Then he grabbed one of Edar's scalpels.

Without pause, Roark plunged the scalpel deep

into the carotid artery.

Edar/Thomas turned in surprise, holding his hand to his neck as blood sprayed Roark in the face and the north wall's specimens. He took a few steps and collapsed.

Roark turned him over. Edar tried to reach for him, but his hands were weak.

"May the Waters of Resurrection wash you clean," Roark said.

A tear rolled down Edar/Thomas's cheek. The part of the person who was Thomas looked up at Roark in gratitude. He had been freed.

"I can no longer go to the Waters of Resurrection," Edar whispered, his dying eyes filled with fear.

Roark grabbed a two-gallon empty jar and slipped it over Edar's head. Edar gasped his last breaths.

As his soul left his body, Roark snapped the jar shut. "I'm sorry, my friend."

Roark wiped his hands down his face and stared at the jar with the swirling mist glimmering inside. He could smash it, but he couldn't bring himself to destroy it. More to the point, because he smashed the jar didn't mean the soul would die. Edar could not face the Waters of Resurrection. What would happen? Would he haunt this cottage? Port Denwort? Roark himself? Who knew?

He caused Edar so much pain in the transmutation ritual. He wished any of his friends were available to advise him. He didn't trust Corwin. He didn't even trust the quartz around his neck. It hadn't brought him wisdom but led him into this mess with Edar and Corwin. Maybe Roark had no business in the Guild. He certainly wasn't wise enough to be a necromancer.

"Goddess, I miss Alana." He thought of the look in Thomas's eyes as he cried out for his mother and Edar whose mother had been an inspiration for his life's work. Alana wasn't his mother, but she had been the person who protected and guided him. And he betrayed her. He ripped the quartz from his neck, leaving a red mark and tossed it upon Edar's exam table.

✻

Chapter 21
Port Denwort
in the Realm of Dynion

ROARK NO LONGER CARED IF THE WHOLE OF Dynion was taken over by a new species; he wanted to escape. He dashed upstairs, pumped water, cleaned himself off as well as he dared. Still, he wouldn't leave *The Great Work* behind, and he had to ensure he took it legally.

He sprinted to the mayor's House. The routine niceties annoyed him, slowing his pace, forcing him to catch his breath. He didn't want to catch his breath; he wanted to get out of Port Denwort. His master was dead; he wanted to see the Expanse and know freedom.

Once inside and facing the mayor, Roark said, "We failed, Mayor Kleidmacher. Edar and Thomas are dead."

The mayor's wizened jaw twitched. His eyes held glimpses of anger, defeat, guilt, and a hint of relief. He scratched his grizzled chin then met Roark's eye. "It was a long shot anyway. Enjoy your youth before it's gone."

"Yes, Mister Mayor."

"And, Lord Roark, I wouldn't have hurt your horse. It pains me that you thought I would."

"Forgive me, but I wasn't sure." Roark stood and bowed.

"Your aunt would kill me if I laid a hand upon you

or yours. Edar must have been in dire need to try, but no one is mayor for fifty years by being a fool. Remember that."

Yet, Roark thought, *there is no wisdom in this house either.* "May I have Edar's notes?"

"And his equipment I suppose."

"Yes. And I'll dispose of anything that would make it hard to lease the cottage."

The mayor laughed. "So, you do have some of your aunt in you. Good to know. Just take the equipment."

Roark thanked the mayor. He left the towering stone house and made his way past the town square. He wasn't ready to face the jar which held Edar's soul or the darkness of the workroom any longer. Just the thought of it caused dread to clamber into his chest and icy sweat to drip under his arms and down his back. Better to be in the daylight.

Feeling the warmth of the sun on his shoulders, he wandered to the sandy beach and drifted to the riverbed watching the small current shape the shore. When he was a boy, Roark believed if he squinted, he could see to the next Realm. His sister told him that it was sea mists making mirages on the horizon. She was correct, of course, but her words made his world a little less magical.

He lifted a large rock and saw several tiny crabs scurry from the sunlight. He gently set the rock back. If two adults couldn't both live in the same form, perhaps an infant would provide the shelter an old soul would need.

He shuddered at the thought, but *The Great Work* pulled him to continue. With hope and dread he would find an abandoned child, Roark roamed the beach.

A faint mewing drew him near a private dock. Below, he found a cat with several kittens, their eyes were open, playing together between the rocks and sand.

One was white with black paws, he recalled his vision. Kian had a cat that looked like that. *What if it was Edar?*

He left the cat and continued on to the town proper to find a fishmonger.

"Have you any old scraps?" Roark asked.

"You sure you want scraps, elf?" The man spoke slowly as if Roark didn't understand the language of Dynion. "Over here is fresh fish. Best fish."

Roark nodded. "Need to tame a cat."

"I know a man with cats. Better cats than you find on the street. Buy a cat already trained and you can eat fresh fish."

"Just the old fish, please."

The wetness soaked his tunic. The rotting fish was sure to smell up his clothes. Maybe he would burn them.

❄

ROARK BOWED TO THE MOTHER CAT WHO eyed him suspiciously as he shuffled closer. "I'm sorry to cause you pain. May this ease your sorrow."

He placed the fish on the ground. The cat sniffed it and left her kittens to play. He gently gathered the white-pawed black kitten and left.

"By taking you, I ensure your brothers and sisters will live better." Roark gently ran his hand along its back, but he didn't believe it.

The kitten purred in response. Roark didn't know if the mother cat would weep over the loss of a single kitten or what the cat even felt, but his heart felt buried in guilt.

He opened the garden gate and carried the kitten into the kitchen. Roark poured the kitten a dish of milk. The feline purred contentedly the entire time he lapped it up. Roark found a large wooden box and put a layer of dry sand at the bottom and set the kitten inside with his milk.

Roark carefully packed each of Edar's machines in fresh straw. He copied each spell, each entry of Edar's work into his own newly purchased journal. Then packed Edar's tome.

In his mind's eye, Roark felt Edar watching him from the jar. Stuck in a body that cannot speak. How long should Roark keep him there? He wanted to walk away again, go upstairs into the light, but he must finish it.

Roark cast a circle of protection around the jar. He donned the mirrored amulet and then carefully opened the lid enough to drop the kitten inside.

"Spirit of Edar Candlewick, enter this form."

Dark mist swirled around the kitten who pawed at the glass and mewed. The soul of Edar slid into its open mouth.

Roark pulled the kitten from the jar and set it on the work table. He kneeled down to meet its golden eyes and said, "I'm sorry, I didn't know what else to do. Are you there?"

The kitten took a feather in its mouth and scrawled onto a parchment "Here." Then the kitten played with the feather.

"We could try again."

"You first."

Roark carefully created a blood potion and mixed it in with another dish of milk and small bits of fish. Once the bowl was licked clean, Roark tucked the kitten into his tunic and put up a sign.

Apothecary Retired. For interest in this property, please contact Mayor Kleidmacher's office.

✳

Chapter 22
Guild House of Olentir
in the Realm of Fairhdel

ROARK LUGGED THE CRATE DOWN THE LONG corridor with the kitten on his shoulder. He could have asked for assistance from a guard or a mechanic. He didn't want help. He wanted to feel the strain on his arms, the splinters in his hands and the ache of his back. Corwin opened the red door to his private meeting room and depository as Roark struggled through.

"So, the original soul overtook the trespasser," he asked, not even hiding his giddiness.

"Yes, House Master."

"And you feel it is not a viable option?"

"It is not a viable option, House Master."

Roark took a step forward and bumped his hip into the wooden table. The pain shot through his leg and into his aching heart. When he looked at Corwin's face, he saw how old and weak it was. He hated the Guild's hypocrisy. Roark slowly opened the crate of instruments. "I brought these."

"Bring them below."

Roark could imagine several places he'd rather be than below in the Guild Vaults. Yet, he followed the House Master a stride behind.

"Did you know Edar would fail?" Roark asked, careful of his footing on the narrow stone stairs.

"I believed he would succeed. And to a certain extent, he did." Corwin gestured to a case marked 741.

Roark stacked the instruments on the tall bookcase and Corwin took down descriptions of each. "The brass alone is worth hundreds. I'll see the cost of the brass is deposited into your accounts. And when you are ready to start again, these will be returned to you."

Roark didn't know if he'd ever be ready. He turned from the case. "Yes, House Master."

Corwin lifted the quartz pendant out of the crate and held it to the light orb. "Did it not guide you well?"

"No, I don't believe it did. It took something from me, something more than blood."

"I feared as much. So much illegal technology is littering the Seven Realms. I've another job for you. Come."

Roark gulped the ever-freshening air as they climbed the steps. "What of the Eighth Realm Beings?"

"Byronia and several human Guild members are still doing reconnaissance. We must tread lightly now, we don't want to start a war with a new species if they come in peace."

"From what I saw they came to dance, play, and drink wine."

"That may be. The truth is we don't know. We don't even know if they truly are from an Eighth Realm. Wars have been fought, and people died over hasty actions."

"But people are dying... the rash ... "

"The Guild will take Edar's first remedies and mix it with others until we find a true remedy—just ensure you always use lambsheads when hiring whores."

Roark's breath felt shallow as his heart dropped into his stomach. "We were never able to find a salve for the rash. The entire experiment was a failure."

"Was it?" Corwin asked. "I learned many things about you, the Eighth Realm beings, the possibility of transmutation, and some common combinations that don't work."

Roark's heart sank lower. "Is my aunt in residence?"

"Going to run to Auntie?"

"Just for advice. I lose my sense of direction when I project away from my body. Especially if I'm inside and unable to see a landmark." Roark sprinkled truth in his words, so Corwin didn't hear the lie.

The light behind Corwin illuminated his wiry white hair and white robes as he snatched the kitten off Roark's shoulder and smacked him across the head with the dossier.

"I will allow you to continue your research between jobs, but don't defy me, Roark, or I will put you in the darkness until madness takes you."

"I'm not a boy any longer and tire of your threats. Please return my cat."

"I do so only because it pleases me."

Corwin placed the dossier in Roark's hands, then set the kitten on top of the folder and gestured for him to leave. "I believe your aunt is in the library."

Ignoring Corwin's ridicule and clutching Edar to his chest, Roark left the cell and raced down the corridor, half expecting Guild guards to capture him and bring him below to the eternal darkness or perhaps just crucifixion. No one stopped him.

※

ROARK WAS STILL TREMBLING WHEN HE came to the entrance of the library. He leaned on the stonewall and listen to the soft ruffle of paper and voices from within. He set Edar on the floor and wiped his face with a handkerchief. He checked his compact and smoothed his clothes. Watching the kitten play with a stray bit of dust, Roark decided it would be best if he stayed in the hall.

Inside, Alana instructed Kian on Larcian grammar. Kian chewed on his thumbnail as he scribbled something on a slate. At a nearby table, Eohan read scrolls. His brow showed he was deep in thought. It felt good to see something normal for a change.

His aunt glanced up from Kian's slate and smiled at Roark. Kian peeked over his shoulder. He jumped to his feet and set his slate on the table. Ignoring his lessons completely, he crossed the room, chalk in hand and clasped Roark's forearm. Thirteen still wasn't kind to Kian, but he looked different somehow. More at peace.

"I can hit the target at thirty paces, blindfolded," he said.

"Hey, that's wonderful," Roark returned the gesture.

"How have you been?" Kian said.

"I've been good," he answered automatically. Then frowned. "No, I haven't. I came to ask my aunt for advice. I'm so glad to see you all."

Once Kian released his arm, Eohan greeted Roark in the same fashion. "Can we help? What's with the cat?"

The kitten had followed him, playing with the edge of his cloak. Roark set the kitten on the table. He made a little sneeze and pounced upon the edge of a tome.

"I don't know." Failure piled upon Roark's heart as he looked at his aunt's calm but withered face. She kissed him on the cheek.

He might have made her young. She might have fought on forever. She would have defeated this new enemy whose very hair was a weapon, but she was old now. Her best option was to teach Eohan to take her place.

"Why are you sad?" Alana said.

"I must speak with you, Auntie." Roark's heavy

arms hung at his sides.

The four sat down at the table where the kitten had found its own tail. Roark quickly explained everything that happened, leaving out Corwin's part entirely. He waited for his aunt to denounce him, to strip him of his title or to call a guard and ask for his crucifixion.

She did not do anything except clasp her hands together and nod. "Edar chose his fate."

"He didn't choose to be a cat," Roark said.

"No, he preferred your body, but thankfully, dearling, you haven't been lax in your training. I only have one question: why were you not armed?"

"He was lonely, and I was too. Byronia was never unarmed; I should've taken her example," Roark said.

Alana put her arm around his shoulders. "I'll take Edar home. There may be a cure, there may not be, but your sister has a gentle heart. She'd keep him safe, and little Saray will ensure he won't be lonely."

"I could snap its neck." Eohan stared at the kitten with hate. "If this is truly Edar Candlewick's soul, let it roam the Realms for eternity."

"No," Alana ordered in her calm way. "Edar can't hurt anyone in this form, except maybe the page of that book." She picked up the kitten whose little teeth had created a hole in the paper. "Do one of you boys have a ribbon or a bit of string on you?"

"A bit of string?" Eohan growled.

Kian rolled his eyes. "It's a kitten, Han." He pulled the ribbon from his hair and let his shoulder-length locks fall. He dangled it in front of the kitten's face. The kitten pounced on the edge of the fabric—as kittens were known to do. Roark wondered if Edar was still in there or if the soul which was the kitten had taken over.

Eohan slammed the book shut. The kitten hissed and jumped from the table to Roark with his tiny claws expanded. He stuck to Roark's tunic and crawled upwards. Roark unstuck him from the wool and held him in his arms.

"Why are you defending Edar Candlewick?" Eohan roared.

At first, Roark believed his friend's anger was directed at him, but Eohan shoved his finger towards Kian.

"He bought you off a slave block and sold you for a silk suit!" Rage rose up Eohan's strained neck to his cheeks, but Kian sat straighter and matched that fury.

"I'm not defending him. This is just one of Lady Alana's stupid tests. Besides what happened, happened to me, not you. I paid the price for this life you love so much."

Eohan's eyes opened wide as if Kian had slapped him.

Roark glanced at Alana. Her thin-lipped expression told him the two brothers quarreled before and most likely would again.

"Eohan, dear, calm yourself," Alana said, "This kitten bares the soul of the man who bought your brother. Every soul goes somewhere. We don't punish for the sins of a past life. For which we should all be glad. I've transgressed many times and so will you."

"But he didn't go through the Water of Resurrection," Eohan shouted. "Roark put him into a jar and then into that creature."

Though he stood a head taller than their venerable master and outweighed her by ten stone, she fixed her icy eyes upon him. "You're to care for this kitten. If I hear so much as a whimper of pain, I will dismiss you. A War Ender never loses their temper."

"I told you it was a stupid test," Kian muttered and shook his head. He gently took the kitten from Roark's hands. "Edling will be fine."

"Edling?" Eohan asked. "Good gods, when will

this end?"

"It's a cat, Han," Kian said. "If I can let my hate go in order to think clearly, so can you. Edling is just a kitten."

As if to prove his species, the kitten mewed.

※

ACKNOWLEDGMENTS

I've written about the history of *The Chronicles of the Martlet,* so I won't repeat myself too much except to say *The Assassin's Twisted Path* was part of my first rewrite. This is one of the reasons it seemed to come out so fast. In the series, this is the first book that I knew from beginning to end.

As always, first of all, I would like to thank my darling husband for always believing in me.

I would also like to thank my editor, Joe Dacy II.

I would like to thank my writing groups for believing in the project and to thank my friends at Two Hour Transport, since I started reading this novel aloud before it was edited.

I would also like to thank my fans who support my endeavors. Whether I know you online or from a convention, without you none of this would be possible.

ABOUT THE AUTHOR

Much to her chagrin, Elizabeth Guizzetti discovered she was not a cyborg and growing up to be an otter would be impractical, so she began writing stories. Guizzetti currently lives in Seattle with her husband and two dogs. When not writing, she loves hiking and birdwatching.

ALSO BY ELIZABETH GUIZZETTI

Comics published by ZB Publications

Faminelands
Out For Souls&Cookies!
Lure

Fantasy published by ZB Publications

The Grove
Chronicles of the Martlet

Science Fiction published by 48Fourteen

Other Systems
The Light Side of the Moon

Illustrations published by Apocalypse Ink

A is for Apex
written by Jennifer Brozek

The Prince of Artemis V
written by Jennifer Brozek

www.ingramcontent.com/pod-product-compliance
Lightning Source LLC
Chambersburg PA
CBHW030536130626
46552CB00006B/2291